DUKLA

OTHER WORKS BY ANDRZEJ STASIUK IN ENGLISH TRANSLATION

White Raven
Tales of Galicia
Nine
Fado
On the Road to Babadag

DUKLA

ANDRZEJ STASIUK

TRANSLATED AND WITH AN INTRODUCTION BY
BILL JOHNSTON

DALKEY ARCHIVE PRESS
CHAMPAIGN • DUBLIN • LONDON

Originally published in Polish as *Dukla* by Wydawnictwo Czarne, Wolowiec, 1999
Copyright © 1997 by Andrzej Stasiuk
Translation and introduction copyright © 2011 by Bill Johnston
First edition, 2011

Library of Congress Cataloging-in-Publication Data

Stasiuk, Andrzej, 1960-
  [Dukla. English]
 Dukla / Andrzej Stasiuk ; translated and with an introduction by Bill Johnston. -- 1st
ed.
     p. cm.
 "Originally published in Polish as Dukla by Wydawnictwo Czarne, Wolowiec, 1999."
 ISBN 978-1-56478-687-6 (pbk. : alk. paper)
 I. Johnston, Bill, 1960- II. Title.
 PG7178.T28D8513 2011
 891.8'538--dc23
                    2011021844

Partially funded by a grant from the Illinois Arts Council, a state agency, and by the
University of Illinois at Urbana-Champaign

This publication has been funded by the Book Institute—the ©POLAND Translation
Program

www.dalkeyarchive.com

Cover: design and composition by Danielle Dutton
Printed on permanent/durable acid-free paper and bound in the United States of America

CONTENTS

TRANSLATOR'S INTRODUCTION

"I'd always wanted to write a book about light," Stasiuk tells us in *Dukla*. And in fact that is precisely what he has done. In achingly beautiful prose, he takes on the quixotic task of rendering in language the experiences we receive through our eyes. At one level, this is how to read *Dukla*—as an extended series of attempts to put into words the different effects of light, and a meditation on what this undertaking entails.

At the same time, of course, a book about light also has to be a book about darkness. *Dukla* is filled with the constant presence of dark, shadows, blackness, night—Stasiuk strains the resources of language to breaking point in striving to convey the absence of light as well as its presence. His goal of "describing light" recalls Claude Monet's desire to *paint* light in his series paintings, though the intense play of light and shade in *Dukla* is reminiscent of nothing so much as Caravaggio's thunderous chiaroscuro.

Yet, extraordinary as this goal is, and however remarkable its results, *Dukla* is also much more than a book about light. In Poland it is widely regarded as Stasiuk's most brilliant achievement and as one of the landmark texts of the postcommunist period. What is it that makes the book so unusual and memorable?

Part of the answer lies in the sheer originality of form. By making light his central organizing principle, Stasiuk is able to play merry havoc with genre. Quite consciously and deliberately, he intertwines memoir, travelogue, and nature writing, together with an admixture of reportage and latter-day ethnography, all subordinated to the wistful discipline of a languid prose poem. Part of the delight of reading *Dukla* is the reader's constant struggle to figure out what exactly it is he or she is reading: what kind of text is this, and how is it to be categorized and thus understood? As in the case of much great literature, with *Dukla* this question has no simple answer, but the multiple resonances of the various genres mentioned above have the effect of weaving the text into the complex fabric of literature itself.

It is also striking that Stasiuk dwells on things and places no one else thinks worthy of writing about. Polish literature has preponderantly been urban in character; writing set in the countryside has traditionally involved country estates, and has concerned above all the life of the gentry. What goes on in the small towns and villages has, with a few notable exceptions (like Wiesław Myśliwski's

Stone upon Stone), been overlooked. Stasiuk goes looking for his poetry, his light and its effects, in precisely those seemingly banal and uninteresting places that others have ignored. One of the gifts this book offers is a new way of looking at the everyday, and learning how to let it captivate us. Even during the papal visit described in Part III of the novella-length "Dukla," what interests Stasiuk is not the pontiff himself so much as the people who come to see him and hear him—the little old lady to whom "the world has suddenly come," or the farmers who have to leave early because, presumably, their cows need milking.

As he enters imaginatively into the lives of these overlooked others and their habitations, Stasiuk displays stunning powers of observation. He is the poet of the concrete; eschewing the general (because "everything that's general ends up on the trash heap"), he is interested in things, objects, tangible items, confident that if he renders them with sufficient clarity and respect they themselves will reveal their meaning. He is a shining vindication of Flaubert's dictum that "anything becomes interesting if you look at it long enough." The brilliant depiction of a rural home in Part II of "Dukla," for instance, is at once a carefully observed catalog of possessions, and a detailed portrait of a moral habitus, to use Pierre Bourdieu's term. It tells us what people are like, what their values and tastes are, through an exquisite presentation of the apparently banal objects they gather around them.

It might be more accurate to say that *Dukla* is about light *remembered*, and in this sense it is also a book about memory. Stasiuk has said elsewhere, in *Fado*, that he is not interested in the future (which he dismisses as "the refuge of fools"), only in the past, which "treats us with seriousness." In *Dukla* he mines his own past, giving us among other things a plaintive evocation of childhood summers spent with his grandparents, and an equally poignant narrative of his erotic awakening as a teenager. And as with every other facet of the book, these recollections are shot through with qualities of light that help transfix them in memory.

In almost every paragraph of this book, Stasiuk displays his extraordinary talent for metaphor and imagery. A man sitting motionless in a bar is like "one of those people who resemble mineral matter"; motorcycles converted into farming vehicles move across a field "like docile beasts of a newly domesticated species"; a dead stork in a meadow looks "like an overturned plaything." Such examples spill from his pen, and are put at the service of a mind that sees things in strikingly original ways. Stasiuk's originality extends to the very language he uses: a couple of years ago, in a workshop in Poland, I showed a group of young people an anonymous passage from an as-yet unpublished novel; within a sentence or two the majority of those present had identified it correctly as being by Andrzej Stasiuk. Part of the joy of reading *Dukla* is knowing that you are listening to a distinct, unmistakable, compelling voice.

Everyone I know who has read *Dukla* has a favorite passage. One friend remembers best the astonishing image of the teenage protagonist entering the skin of the dancing woman he is watching, pushing his hands into her fingertips like putting on a glove. Another recalls the little girl whose swinging feet in a country bus shelter are the only moving thing in sight, till her mother says "Sit still" and the entire scene becomes motionless. Like the exploratory mine shaft that the Polish word "dukla" refers to, *Dukla* the book bores into the surface of our lives and perceptions; it reveals wondrous prospects and resources whose very existence was unsuspected, and sheds dazzling new light on lives and landscapes that each reader will respond to in different and unique ways. This, too, is the pleasure of reading *Dukla*.

BILL JOHNSTON

DUKLA

MIDSUMMER, POGÓRZE

At four in the morning the night slowly raises its dark backside as if it were getting up from a heavy dinner and going to bed. The air's like cold ink, it flows along the road surfaces, spills to each side and congeals into black lakes. It's Sunday and people are still asleep, that's why this story ought to lack a plot, because no one thing can cover up other things when we're headed toward nothingness, toward the realization that the world is merely a momentary obstacle in the free passage of light. Lutcza, Barycz, Harta, Mały Dół, Tatarska Góra: faded green road signs show the way, but in those places nothing is happening, nothing is moving except dreams, which can see in the dark like cats or bats and which keep pacing about, brushing against the walls, the religious pictures, cobwebs, and whatever else people have accumulated over the years. The sun is still hidden deep, it's fretting at another world right now, but in an hour's time it'll rise to the surface, emerge like a beetle crawling out of a piece of wood. The sound of the car engine can probably be heard for miles. The road follows the crest of the hills, dipping then rising again, each time higher and higher, and in that incomplete darkness, between the specters of woods and houses, it feels like a spiral tower.

At this time of day the sky is barely separate from the earth, the boundary between them hasn't yet been fixed; the two are simply different kinds of dark in which the imagination can run wild. Though what can people imagine to themselves, in fact, aside from all the things that others have seen in this place, banal things made from the faint, indistinct forms of reality; this is nothing but a kind of night blindness, an absurd game of Chinese whispers. And the truth of it is that sight touches the dark, cold, damp colors the way a hand strokes smooth satin, the warm lining of an overcoat when it's chilly outside, in the same unthinking way, with the same sense of pleasure.

There won't be any plot, there won't be any story, especially in the night, when the terrain is stripped of its landmarks, when we're driving from Rogi to Równe and on through Miejsce Piastowe. We're traveling between place-names in a solution of pure idea. Reality doesn't put up any resistance, so all stories, all consequences, all the old marriages of cause and effect are uniformly devoid of meaning.

Kombornia. Where do these names come from? It's been so long since the last moment they still had any significance. The puttering sound of the car rising high into the air is like the rattle of a sewing machine. Darkness leaches into the seams, and tacking the journey together does no good whatsoever. The eastern sky-line lightens like a silvery snake that's come to rest stretched out between the peaks of the hills. Its cold hue is a forecast of heat and dust and so we need to get a move on, mount those motion-less waves then plunge down again to the bottom of a desolate ocean where houses shake off the darkness like dogs coming out of water, or stand whitely there like skulls in flashing sunglasses. And that's where all the people are. They're lying on their backs, or on their bellies with their shoulders pointing upward, dreaming their dreams, sweating or calm, covered up or outside a kicked-off mound of sheets, some still in their Saturday clothes. They have no idea someone's thinking about them. Actually they don't even re-ally exist. Their minds are at rest, the sickness that is life has let up temporarily and they're like pieces of heavy fabric—almost lifeless and almost happy. Jan, Stanisław, Florian, Maria, Cecylia—a litany addressed to the old saints. Another minute and time will blow them out like the wind extinguishing a candle. They'll become part of the past and nothing will be a danger to them anymore, no ris-ing dawn, no sweltering day. Shades in the dark.

Domaradz. The mist is joining the sky. It reveals haystacks, black fences, pointed roofs. The air is dark green. A viscid sky detaches itself from the horizon. In the crack, the glow of another world can be seen. Those who were dying imagined that this was where they were going.

*

Midsummer, Pogórze, the dawn is taking air into its lungs and each successive outbreath is brighter. For another hour it'll still be possible to imagine the lives of other people. It's that dead time when the world is gradually becoming visible but is as yet unpopulated. The light has the hue of melted silver. It's weighty. It spreads along the skyline but does not illuminate the earth. Down here semidarkness and inference still reign, objects are no more than their own shadows. The sky is bursting with the glow, but it remains trapped inside like air in a child's balloon. The people lie in their houses and the story of each one of them could move in any direction if it weren't for fate, which lives with them under the same roof and has a certain number of possibilities up its sleeve, but never oversteps itself. The saints watch over them from their pictures, eternally vigilant, motionless, already having done all they had to do. Their idealized visages are mirrors that time in its purest form now rubs up against. It's undisturbed by any gesture, any deed. This is what heaven is like: life does exist there, but just in case, it never takes on any form.

I ought to be a ghost, I ought to enter their homes and seek out everything they have to hide. The imagination is powerless. All it does is repeat things it's seen and heard, repeat them in an altered voice, attempt to commit sins that were already committed long ago.

Another moment and daybreak will rise higher, dogs will be seen standing by their kennels or at the roadside, but not barking. At this time of day smell and hearing slowly lose significance, while sight hasn't yet acquired it, so it's best to treat everything as if it were a dream, a figment of the doggy imagination. A cat is crouching on the windowsill of a brick-built house. It's chosen the place where the first rays of the sun will fall.

There'll be no plot, with its promise of a beginning and hope of an end. A plot is the remission of sins, the mother of fools, but it melts away in the rising light of the day. Darkness or blindness give things meaning, when the mind has to seek out a way in the shadows, providing its own light.

Already it's bright enough to see fences, trees, trash, junk-filled yards, broken-down cars sinking into the dirt and disintegrating patiently like minerals; pickets, stakes, slim cold chimneys, shafts of carts, motorbikes with lowered heads, outhouses lurking around corners, telegraph poles festooned with cables that droop in mourning, a spade stuck into the ground and forgotten—all this is there, in its place, but none of these things yet casts a shadow, though the sky to the east resembles a silver looking glass; the brightness is reflected in it but remains invisible. This must have been what the world looked like just before it was set in motion: everything was ready, objects poised on the threshold of their destinies like people paralyzed by fear.

*

A couple of months ago R. and I drove through here together. It was the middle of the day, April, we were headed in the opposite direction. Snow lay among the trees. The clouds were standing in place, the light was rarefied and immobile, it yielded before the eye, and the farthest ridges, houses, spiked rows of trees were as distinct as objects close by, just slightly reduced in size. We didn't meet any other cars, no people could be seen. One time a face appeared briefly at a dark window. Yellowish, waterlogged meadows dropped downward from the hill; at the bottom of the valley they were taken in by the swollen river. Stillness hovered everywhere. Lace curtains in windows, closed doors, wickets, farmyard gates, deserted bus stops, there wasn't even a single stupid chicken. The only things moving were us, the water down below, and the tatters of smoke hanging over the cottages. The landscape, unpeopled to its furthest limits, looked like a stage set on which something was going to take place only later, or else already had. The entire area was dominated by space, it filled every nook and corner of the world like liquid glass. We were talking. But there were people in every one of the houses and I kept losing track of what we were saying, because all of them, children, women, men, they all had names and blood flowed in them from head to toe, and even though they couldn't be seen they were all living their own lives. Dozens of them, hundreds, along the whole route thousands of bodies and souls, each one trying in its own way to cope with the day. They were sitting around tables, stoves, televisions. Their heads were populated with all the people they'd ever known or remembered. The people they knew and remembered had their own people, and those people had theirs . . . R. and I were talking but I kept losing the thread of the conversation, because infinity always inspires awe.

From time to time a wind blew up and pushed the clouds along; snow would begin to fall, then melt at once. It was Maundy Thursday, and we were taking the long way back from Jarosław. We'd wanted to see Przemyśl, but there'd been a blizzard there, the green road signs had been covered in snow and the only thing we'd visited was the cold inside of a corner shop in some village on the outskirts. R. bought a mineral water and I got something else because we were both really thirsty. We got clear of the whiteness, it tossed a few handfuls after us but we were quicker than it.

The way in front of us was light, far, empty. Life had no intention of showing itself. The hills, houses, water, clouds all had the distinctness of a supernatural photograph. In a landscape like that, thoughts sound like mechanical music. You can watch them, listen to them, but their meaning is always ominous, like echoes in a well. The glass dome of the sky was tightly closed over the earth; the air was receding, making way for pure space, and our journey, the movement of the car, was becoming less and less self-evident.

*

But now it's midsummer, Dynów is coming up soon, and I'm remembering this road from a year ago when W. and I drove this way. Haystacks ascended the hills in single file, vanished over crests, and reappeared again on the next rise, till in the end they were engulfed by the green darkness. Because it was evening, Saturday evening into the bargain. Young men were swaggering along the side of the road, night was coming out to meet them and was so immense that each of them thought they'd see all their dreams come true. Under trees, outside little stores, or in orchards there were plastic tables and chairs. They looked like herds of diminutive skeletons. People were drinking Leżajsk beer or sticky fruit wine instinct with hotness. The women were sitting with their arms folded, the men were gesticulating, the children ate potato chips and formed their own circles—precise miniatures of the adults' leisure time. White and red Prince parasols, blue and white Rothmans ones, crimson to the west, in the east a darkened blue. Dirt roads led down from the hills toward the main road. People were coming down them on their way for a night out. Their white shirts were bright as sails, or phantoms. We were driving slowly. The whole place must have looked like a moving map, it seemed like no one had stayed home, though windows were lit up with the gray glow of television sets. Perhaps the TVs were waiting alone in empty living rooms, like faithful dogs. Leżajsk beer and wine viscid from the heat. The young guys were disappearing in the darkness, girls stood for a moment longer in the ring of light then vanished too. Through the windows of stores the shop girls could be seen in their regular clothes. Their aprons had already been thrown in the laundry. It was a sultry twilight carnival, as the dark hour advanced from the bushes and orchards. That's where night assembles before it heads out into the world, while they were entering into it, vanishing, passing through the gloom one by one, lighting the way with their cigarettes, and meeting up somewhere in its heart, far from view. The windows of the car were rolled down. I could smell that smell, I was like a dog that could think.

The air stood still in the squares in front of churches. It was as if the entire emptiness of the world had gathered in exactly those places. A little mongrel ran diagonally across the dry, trampled earth, a church spire rose slowly into the sky, which was dropping lower and lower, and the dog, its living presence, seemed a caprice, a tiny piece of madness brought here from some other time. All around, in the depths of space that had been warmed during the day, people were burrowing passageways for themselves like worms in cheese, and in church courtyards the silence and chill were forming into something that resembled large, irregularly shaped aquaria.

W. was driving cautiously, because Saturday evenings are filled with apparitions. People separate into their selves and their longings, emanate their own half-visible likenesses so the latter might try all forbidden things. The boys resembled their own dreams as they strutted along the side of the road on the lookout for girls, who were trying on dresses earlier that day, but in the mirror the fabric of their outfits became invisible and they found themselves looking at their own naked bodies. Moving at thirty miles an hour, we passed through air that was dense as water and filled with proliferating reflections, cloudy spots, and waves. Somewhere close to Dubiecko the sky finally joined with the earth and night fell for good.

*

All these journeys are like transparent slides. They're superimposed upon one another like stereoscopic photographs, but this doesn't make the picture any deeper or clearer. Light can't be described, all that can be done is to keep imagining it afresh. A man in a drab shirt and denim overalls comes out of a house and heads toward the stable. Seven seconds. That's it. We're already further on. It's quite possible that during that night he made a baby, it's possible he'll manage to lead the horse out to pasture and then, smoking his first cigarette of the day, he'll die. An untold number of past beings came together to make up his existence, and each of them was the size of the whole world. Reality is nothing more than an indefinite number of infinities. Then the child in the womb adds its own and everything starts again from yet another beginning. Seven seconds before he disappeared around the red brick corner. The story is motionless and offers protection from madness.

The shadows of early morning lie upon the earth as if the wind were blurring them. They're black yet hazy, because the dew atomizes the light and refracts it at the edges. Even in the middle, the black is far from distinct—it rather resembles a reflection. Beyond Dynów the San touches up against the road with its crooked elbow. We have to flip down the visor, because the sun is shining directly in our eyes. It hangs there just above the road. The blacktop is peeling like old gilding. The river down below has the color of a mirror in an unlit room. For the moment the brightness remains high up in the air, and the future is probable but by no means certain. Before Dubiecko we pass a car. We see its black belly and four wheels in the air. It looks like an animal that wants to play. The cops have their hands in their pockets as if the whole business is over. The blue flashing light on the police car rotates helplessly in the luminous morning air. A few rubbernecks crane over the fence by the ditch. As they stare they smoke cigarettes, we see the blue smoke. This kind of stillness always sets in at a place of death. The sun is rising ever higher, so people can take a look at their world.

DUKLA

We got there in the afternoon. People were standing on the street corners waiting for something. It was quiet, there was hardly any traffic; the men were smoking and the women talked in subdued voices. A policeman in a white shirt told us it was the funeral of a long-serving firefighter.

Whenever I'm in Dukla, there's always something happening. The last time it was that frosty December light at dusk. There was an intense blue drifting in the air. It was invisible but tangible and firm. It descended onto the rectangular market square and solidified there like frozen water. The town hall was embedded in a block of fine ice that sharpened the edges of its tower and topmost story, and the people had had the foresight to go elsewhere. After all, what lifeless stone can bear may be harmful for the body. The shadows passing from time to time along the walls belonged to drunks. The shadows were warm inside and so were in no danger. But all the same, none of them dared to take a shortcut, crossing the market square diagonally and entering that glassy, sonorous zone.

And now this funeral. The procession came up Cergowska Street, brushed against the firehouse, and turned into Węgierski Trakt, where it spread out in the sun like a colorful, indolent snake, an anaconda, or like a gigantic centipede. A black church pennant fluttered at the front; then came other colors; the dark casket swayed on the shoulders of six firefighters in gold helmets. It's hard to recall the order, but after that I believe there came the priest, the altar boys, and a band with trumpets glinting like the helmets; the trombonist had a long ponytail tied with an elastic band dangling beneath his fireman's cap. That's how it was. Oh, and the widow following behind the casket, with the family and the dignitaries. And then a caravan of fire trucks: Żuks; Tatras with three ladders; Jelczes; UAZs, all red as the hottest fire; and at the very end a Star 25, an ancient model from perhaps thirty years before, but still alive, bright and plucky. It looked like a toy that had grown up. When they crossed Mickiewicza, the bells of Mary Magdalene and of the Cistercian monastery started up, and the vehicles turned on their sirens. The two laments, sacred and secular, intertwined, unraveling only when they were high in the sky, and it was so sublime and beautiful that D. and I stood dumb-struck, not saying a word, though I'm certain that like me he was thinking how good it would be to have a funeral like that one day. The plaintive wailing hovered over the town; cars pulled over onto the sidewalks and police officers instinctively and spontaneously stood to attention. Behind the cavalcade of fire trucks there were just regular citizens. And if the town of Dukla numbers about two thousand inhabitants, at least half of them were accompanying the casket to the cemetery, while the other half watched the procession. Because the market square was once again deserted and sweltering, and only the dust and a single cyclist were attempting to do something with that rectangular void covered by a light blue lid of sky. This was around the beginning of May. Then we drove off toward Komańcza, the sun shining at our backs.

And I keep going back to Dukla to observe it in different kinds of light and different seasons. For example, the time in July when the sky was enveloped in the oppressive milky glow of stormy weather. The bottle of beer I drank in the tourist-office bar instantly made itself felt on my skin. I was alone, and I thought to myself I'd take a good close look at it all so as to finally grasp the spirit of the place and capture the scent that I was always sure existed, because places and towns give off smells like animals; you just have to keep looking till you hit on the right trail and find its hiding place. You have to attack it at different times of the day and night and when tedium throws you out the door, you have to try from another direction, through the window or along the road from Żmigród or from Bóbrka, until there's the kind of miracle that makes light bend in the uncanniest way and eventually weave into a transparent fabric that for a split second blocks out the world; at such times you stop breathing as if before death, but no fear comes.

Dukla then, a handful of crisscrossed streets, one church, one monastery, and the shell of a synagogue in which stunted birch trees cling to the wall several feet above ground level. It was Sunday and in front of the church of Mary Magdalene the priest was blessing a bevy of freshly washed cars. A short distance away some Ukrainians had spread out their wares on the hoods of dusty Zhygulis and, arms folded, were regarding this pagan ceremony. Their vehicles covered great distances without any benediction. Their goods were shoddy and the elegant faithful passed them by with an air of superiority. On Sunday, objects become a little less real, and temptation trots at your heel like a dog. They were mostly tools—drills, hammers, saws, metalworking implements—so it was hardly surprising that right after High Mass they looked a little blasphemous. No one was buying anything and the people from Lviv or Drohobych stood there immobile, immersed in the milky glare of the unseen sun, lost in their waiting like true easterners who suspect that time has no end, so you need to be sparing with the gestures life is performed with, to make them last as long as possible.

I walked along 3 Maja. A chalky light sprinkling from above blurred the shadows. People were separate, solitary, quiet. Before a storm the air is dense and soft. In the greenish waters of the Dukielka nothing was reflected. To the right, stacked on one another were gardens, sheds, and the rear walls of small apartment buildings, which on the side overlooking the market square were smooth and pastel-colored, calling to mind a confectionery contest. Over there, pink, greenish pistachio, faded gingerbread brown, and custard cream took on the shapes of bay windows, ornamental borders, cornices, and curved, sagging balconies. But on this side nature had run rampant and despite the fact that it was July the colors of the flowers were vivid as flames, as raspberry juice and sulfur, perhaps because a tongue of river chill licked this special spot in the middle of town. Men in white shirts with rolled-up sleeves could be seen through the open windows. They were sitting down at tables to have a drink and stare into the green depths of the mansion grounds on the far side of the creek, where field artillery and cannons warmed their olive-green armor plating in the half-visible sun.

That was how it was. But this time too I left with nothing.

Just as twenty-some years before I'd left with nothing from my summer vacation, bloated with heat, swollen from the vastness of sky-blue space strung across the plain of the Bug Valley like a trembling, rippling parasol; and it's only now, twenty-some years later, that I'm digesting it all like an old snake, dissolving it in my soul, breaking it down with the juices of memory into its constituent parts, so as to experience their taste and smell; because time is the opposite of space and through its veil things can be seen more and more distinctly, if only because they can never be touched again.

That time we'd been sitting on the hill behind the wooden church. The river down below was gray-green, like a meadow toward the end of summer, and on its other bank, far away at the edge of the sandy flatland, something was on fire in the village of Arbasy. The afternoon weighed heavily on our heads, and the garish brightness prevented the fire from forming into a cockscomb. In the glare-bleached expanse it was little more than a reddish pinprick. Fire's no match for weather. It glowed like a tiny lump of coal, the wind lacked the strength to blow on it and it only carried the distant moan of a fire siren. A black horse was grazing across the river and didn't so much as raise its head. It was a long way off, but I could have sworn its sweat-soaked skin was glistening with the reflected light of the sun. As far as the eye could see there wasn't a single tree. Only on the horizon was there a ribbon of green marked by the pulsing red dot of the blaze.

Then later, in the evening, the mayflies came out in swarms, the place looked like a snowstorm. Millions of creatures swirled around the few streetlamps in the center of the village. The mercuric light dimmed as continual white waves of bugs flew in from the river. The living matter thickened around the glow and eventually a huge, trembling sphere hung around each lamp. The dark air was filled with shadows. It was impossible to tell people from magnified specters of insects. Everything stank of fish and silt. The mayflies danced then fell to earth. Soon, every footstep made a crunching sound. The road looked like it was scattered with living snow. It was only beyond where the streetlights stood that the night had its regular feel and smell.

I remember all this ever more vividly. The distant red point of the fire expands, spreads across the landscape, the faraway space begins to char like paper and from under its flimsy black ash other events show through. They stretch into infinity, like a suite of rooms in a dream.

That night I went back to my uncle and aunt's house. The sandy lane led by an empty place where there'd once been a windmill, though for me it was still there, made from the darkness of the wind, towering over the dusty road, and it would remain there always, though the world would probably turn a good many somersaults, just as it did now when I turned from 3 Maja into Dukla's market square, and just like now, when I'm trying to describe it all, and those onion layers accumulate in the body and in the mind, one showing through beneath another like a shirt under a threadbare sweater, like the skin of someone's backside under well-worn pants. Because the present is weakest of all, it spoils and disintegrates faster than anything.

That night I clambered up to my little attic room in the dark. There was a smell of resinous wood. The boards were radiating the heat they'd absorbed during the long day. I turned on the light. Black ground beetles hid themselves in the cracks of the floorboards. They looked like mobile drops of tar. I could smell them in the heated air.

It's a strange thing that I don't recall any of my thoughts or feelings from that time. I don't remember any of the things that actually were dearest to me, so I have to imagine them to myself. It's exactly as if I were nothing more than an extraneous addition to the world. I don't remember fear, pain, joy. All that comes into my mind are events that could have evoked one or another of these emotions. That's all. Nothing more.

But I ought to go back to Dukla. It appears like an admonition whenever I start thinking about myself too much.

This time was in summer too, August I believe. There was a northerly wind. Swift-moving white clouds were crossing the sky.

The air had the kind of cold transparent hue that offers nothing for the eye to fix on. The cone of Cergowa Mountain looked as if it rose immediately beyond the garden fences, and every little bush, every tree on the crest was as clear as a paper cutout. The clouds alternately hid the sun and uncovered it. Because of this people acquired a double existence, since their shadows kept appearing then vanishing again, and each figure would stand now with a patch of black at its feet, now entirely alone. You had the irresistible sense that the wind was blowing away the dark impressions of bodies from the roadway and that the light, or rather the lack of it, seemed as material as sand. It wasn't just the people, the whole town was given over to this restless, yet, when it came down to it, monotonous transformation. It kept dividing into two, then reconstituting itself again. The play of disappearing shadows revealed the duality of the world with such power that I was expecting the market square to disappear, and with it the squat apartment buildings, the two drunks leaving the hotel bar and entering directly into the emptiness of the afternoon, the town-hall tower, all solid matter, and nothing would remain but the black absence of light, the other side of reality that ordinarily marks only its edges, but now was spilling out, submerging everything in a confusion of shadow that was reaching for what belonged to it like a banished son from a fairy tale returning home after many years, and the town of Dukla would disappear in a crack between dimensions, or the place where the five human senses lose their power and all that's left is a presentiment that the profound, vivid everyday landscape might suddenly turn inside out.

But I saw a sign reading "Kalwaria Furniture" and everything continued on its regular man-made tracks. I cut diagonally across the market square and found myself by the creek, marveling once again at the size of the glassed-in wooden veranda at the back of the building that houses the jeweler's in front, while behind is this miraculous thing the size of a railroad car, suspended over the greenish stream like a rickety hothouse. That day I had a yen to see the mansion. It stood amid greenery, so bright it was almost white, crowned with its black roof. I walked around it, coming from the direction of the playing field that had been abruptly turned into a sodden park. The viscous water of the ponds had probably been there for centuries. A few ducks were trying to swim in it, but they were barely able to move across the stodgy surface, and they left no trace whatsoever of their passage. Darkness condensed in the avenues of lindens. The sun was shining over the area, but here the light disappeared. In the farthest corner, where the wall twisted to the left and mounted the hillside, I met the only person in sight. He was as restive as only an animal can be in a park—squirrel, rabbit, or magpie. He was poking around in the bushes, and even at my discreet remove I could hear him mumbling. I observed his back in its dull-colored jacket for a full minute before I finally realized what he was doing. He was looking for empty plastic Coca-Cola and Sprite and Mirinda bottles, unscrewing their colored caps and sticking them in his pocket. Because at that time you could win a fortune if you found the two matching halves of an amulet. The man cursed every time he found a bottle without a cap. In his right hand he carried a plastic bag filled with these treasures. He noticed me and shuffled off toward the edge of a pond where the wind had gathered a whole flotilla of bottles in a little bay. One of his shoes was black, the other brown. For my part, I was recalling how, two hundred years ago, Jerzy August Wandalin Mniszech issued a decree that imposed upon the good citizens of Dukla the obligation to educate their children. I also remembered that paintings by Lorrain had hung in Mniszech's mansion. I set off in that direction. I passed the chapel, I passed the mansion's cold room, which was now no more than a pile of rocks. From Węgierski Trakt came the hum of cars driving to Krosno or coming back.

For a long time now it's seemed to me that the only thing worth describing is light, its variations and its eternal nature. Actions interest me to a much lesser degree. I don't remember them very well. They arrange themselves in random sequences that break off without reason and begin without cause, only to snap unexpectedly once again. The mind is skilled at patching up, tacking, putting things in order, but I'm not the smartest guy in the world and I don't trust the mind, just like a country bumpkin doesn't trust city folks, because for them everything always arranges itself in neat, deft, illusory series of deductions and proofs. So, light. I quickly reached the end of the vehement dark green glow of the grounds, and set off toward the mansion across the graveled courtyard.

Inside it smelled of turpentine, as museums always do. The lady at the desk sold me a ticket, while an aging dog sniffed at me without interest. I slipped on some felt overshoes and followed the arrow, dragging their long laces behind me. I wanted to track down the Lorrains.

But there was nothing there, nothing but suites of rooms plunged in penumbra and filled with black oxidized weaponry. In the utter stillness and silence the guns looked like ideal and un-used things. A yellowish light seeped from the glass display cases; its color recalled old wood, or a room where someone's forgotten to turn off a night-light. A Goryunov heavy machine gun stood on its wheeled base. Its ribbed barrel widened into a comical funnel, while its two wooden grips were like the handles of old-fashioned flatirons. Next to it, on a spread bipod was a Degtyaryov with a butt like an oar split in half. I tapped the drum of the magazine. It was empty, and only slightly larger than a cookie tin. Under glass there were two Tokarev TT-33 semiautomatic pistols, so-called *tetetkas*, produced in Tula, where the samovars come from, though, unlike those objects, these ones were not in the least shiny. Gray metal showed through beneath the corrosion, and the star in the grip had lost its gleam from fearful or mortal perspiration half a century before. Next to the two Tokarevs lay a Luger, that is to say, a Parabellum P08 with a long barrel. This was the kind of pistol used by German artillerymen, and just as with the commissars' Mauser C96, you could attach a wooden stock. But there was no stock here. The slight grooving of the grip formed a pattern that brought to mind a snake, or fishnet stockings. Next there was an automatic pistol reminiscent of a German Bergmann, then an MP40, and a series of drooping, scarecrowlike uniforms with holes where bullets had passed through. There were also antitank mines and personnel mines, mounds of helmets and bayonets, a Mauser 98 with bulging barrel, unexploded grenades, bullet-holed mess cans from which the smell of spirits had evaporated, ebonite ra-diotelephones veined like marble, a funny-looking MG34 with its binocularlike magazine and its butt like a fishtail, the green cases of radio units with white indicator-eyes whose needles had frozen at certain death-dealing or victorious frequencies, and a thousand other things that had served their purpose and were now to take their rest for all time in this warm and quiet sepulcher where the only sound was the shuffling of my overshoes.

And as I tried to pull back the lock on the Goryunov, I suddenly sensed I wasn't alone. By the doorway of the room, in the lusterless golden light, stood a woman in a dark dress. I expected a telling-off for having dared to touch one of the exhibits, but she merely asked:

"Are you interested in Marshal Piłsudski?"

I couldn't bring myself to give an unambiguous answer, and the woman evidently noticed my hesitation, because she said:

"In that case I'll show you something else. Please, follow me."

We went out onto the staircase. The laces of the felt overshoes scuttled behind me like lizards. The small windows told me we were in the attic. The woman went up to a low, solid door and opened it with a key. I thought of Lorrain.

The new room bore no resemblance to the dark labyrinth that preceded it. It was large and filled with light. Dozens of pictures hung on the walls. My guide stood to one side and observed me closely, waiting for my reaction. I went up to one of the gilt frames. The woman gave me a few seconds, then said: "It's by Mr. —ski, a local master butcher. It's lovely, don't you think?"

Blades of grass and loops of colored yarn had been shaped into an image of the Dukla town hall. It looked like a field of multicolored grass. A hairy blue sky bristled over the white edifice with its angular turret. Subsequent pictures depicted small apartment buildings, the market square, Mary Magdalene church, the Cistercian monastery, all in miraculous pastel shades, unblemished by any shadow, merely outlined in black in a few places, like in a Raoul Dufy, but purer, gaudier, and drenched in sunlight like a red-tinted meadow.

"Are these all by the same gentleman?" I asked.

"They are. Mr. —ski is retired."

Further on there were Orthodox churches and chapels scorched on wood, pictures assembled from straw or colored scraps of material, thick, uneven oil paintings, all showing the beauty of the Dukla region.

The light in Lorrain's pictures is horizontal, horizontal or diagonal. Its source is located somewhere near the skyline and before it reaches the place where the canvas ends and the world begins, it's so weak that it seems to have exhausted itself, burned itself out in that Lorrainian reality. In "Landscape with Dancing Figures" the proscenium is plunged in shadow, making the human figures acquire a double materiality. Their bodies bear the color of the earth. In the depths of the scene the transparent air permeates the forms that are there and the boundary between visible and invisible, real and imagined, is preserved only because of the fallibility of our gaze, which has to be looking at something in order to perceive something. Everything the light falls on is moving toward its own ideal, toward a world made safe by the limitations of our senses. But this is a good thing, as otherwise we'd die of tedium while we were still alive.

So it is. But all this is barely a suspicion. Later, though, when I studied a reproduction of "Landscape with Dancing Figures," the original of which is in some museum in Rome, I noticed that Mount Soracte, which closes the composition, has the exact same shape as Cergowa Mountain. Especially when you're coming from Żmigród. The highway climbs and falls, and with each rise Cergowa emerges higher and higher over the surface of the landscape. It looks like a peak that's straining to tip over. Its north slope is extraordinarily steep, whereas the other faces drop away gently in the usual way of the Beskid mountains. It looks like it's crawling northward, dragging its lumbering, flabby body behind it like a seal, or a man pulling himself along by his elbows.

So then, Cergowa and Soracte, which Lorrain painted many times, and which many times served as the last and most important word in his story. Distant, gray-blue, and irregular like the rest of this world, in which existence is always a caprice of the light.

But it was only much later that I discovered this resemblance. Back in the mansion, we walked along the line of those homespun absurdities in which naïveté mingled with innocence, love with ineptitude, utter barbarity of form with absolute tenderness of content, and I was thinking as usual about time, in other words about a banal and ubiquitous thing, about the bizarre transformation that had swept Lorrain aside and replaced him with a Goryunov, a Shpagin submachine gun, and pictures burned on wood and made with colored threads. And I couldn't figure out what was true, I couldn't fathom the final destination of time, which in Dukla had begun perhaps four hundred years earlier, when it was acquired by the Mniszechs of Moravia, one of whom, George, had even been father-in-law to the tsar. True, it had only been the pretender Grishka Otrepyev: George's daughter Marina had married that mad monk, and then when he was murdered she married False Dmitriy II, swearing by everything holy that he was the miraculously saved False Dmitriy I. When the second Dmitriy was also killed, she took up with the next would-be Emperor of All the Russias, Ivan Zarutsky, a Don Cossack ataman, but that was the end of her monarchical ambitions, because they impaled Ivan, drowned her, and hanged the usurper's three-year-old child. A hundred years later, the mansion at Dukla became home to Maria Amalia, née Brühl, daughter of the Brühl who controlled the scepter of August III and made both Poland and Saxony quake; the daughter equaled her father in intrigue and in deed, dividing her interests equally between Rubens, the theater, and assassination— it was rumored she had had a hand in the drowning of Gertruda Komorowska in the Huczwa River after Gertruda improvidently married Szczęsny Potocki, whom Amalia had picked out as a son-in-law for herself and a husband for her daughter Józefina. That was how it was.

A trace of this madness remained in Maria Amalia's tomb, at Mary Magdalene. Her figure, carved in pink marble, reposes upon the black case of a sarcophagus. Amalia is lying on her back, but her head is tipped to the right as if the dead woman were only sleeping. Her marble clothing is arranged into fanciful, lifelike folds. It looks like crumpled bedding. This Rococo death has something of the boudoir about it. It's quite possible that beneath the pleats of stone Amalia is still warm and that her body has retained the living firmness that comes from a long sleep. In the black sarcophagus upon which the figure rests, her bones are gradually turning into powder, into something ever more mineral, suffused with eternity; they are turning into eternity itself, because in the end the only thing left will be dust rising into the interstellar spaces. But who cares about this dark box, filled with condensed death, even if this death were to manifest itself in the form of the eternal?

I left the mansion and found myself at Mary Magdalene. The church was empty, quiet, and cold; I stood at the tomb and I was in fact fairly sure that beneath the marble covering of her shoes her feet were still warm, and that blood still pulsed under the hard smoothness of her fingernails. After all, this figure hadn't been formed around a lifeless skeleton, no, it had covered the living image of Amalia, her being, which had moved through the mansion at Dukla, plotting, yielding to pleasures and hatreds. This stone had enclosed all the gestures that constituted her from the moment she woke in the morning till the moment she fell asleep at night, all her actions, her sins, and everything else, all the countless places she occupied in space day after day.

So then, I had a desire to touch this cadaverous and at the same time unsettlingly live substance, enter into it, just as one enters the organic integument of a human being by means of violation or love, but I heard steps behind me and an extremely young priest in glasses said softly:

"I'm sorry, but we're closing."

"What if someone wanted to visit right at this moment?" I asked, but he just lowered his eyes and repeated what he had said. He began turning off the lights. I walked away and left the church.

The wind was still blowing. I passed a closed newspaper kiosk. It stood with its back to the church. Copies of *Cats* and *Playstars*, girlie magazines, lay behind the glass. The women's bodies were shiny and still. Their mouths had frozen in "ahs" and "oohs," halfway between mockery and surprise. Death had caught up with them and then immediately abandoned them, as if it didn't have the time, and that was probably why the naked women's eyes were still wide open. A kid with a raspberry-flavored ice cream was staring at them. A trickle of pink had run down the cone and was about to reach his hand. He jumped like someone woken from sleep, glanced at me, and moved over to where there were cosmetics, combs, washing powder. I headed toward the bus station. I examined the yellow sign listing departures. For the next hour there was nothing I could use.

In the dark shelter that resembled a ruined arcade there was a family sitting and waiting for their bus. No one was talking. The children copied the stoical gravity of their parents. The only thing moving were the little girl's legs, which swung rhythmically above the ground in their white stockings and shiny red shoes with golden buckles. In the emptiness of the Sunday afternoon, in the stillness of the bus station, this motion brought to mind the helpless pendulum of a toy clock unable to cope with the burden of time. The girl had slipped her hands under her thighs and was sitting on them. The glistening red weights of her feet were rocking in an absolute vacuum. Nothing was added or taken away by the swinging. It was pure movement in an ideal, purified space. Her mother was staring emptily ahead. A yellow frill bubbled under her dark blue top. The father was leaning forward, his arms resting on his spread knees, and he too was peering into the depths of the day, toward the meeting point of all human gazes that have encountered no resistance on their path. The woman straightened her hands where they lay in her lap and said, "Sit still." The girl froze immediately. Now all of them were gazing into the navel of the afternoon emptiness, and it was all I could do to tear myself from that motionless slumber.

It was then I promised myself I'd never again go to Dukla on a Sunday, when everyone is spending the afternoon at home, while inertia creeps out onto the market square and the streets, and matter manifests itself in its most primal, indolent form, filling every crack and crevice, emptying them of light, air, human traces, even driving time from them in those few hours before evening, before the bars fill up, because in the houses the afternoon has started to make the men feel sick.

Two Slovak cars were lumbering toward Barwinek. Old Skoda one-oh-fives with sagging rear ends. I crossed the roadway and plodded through the gravid Sunday atmosphere. Even the wind was slowly easing off. There was no sign of holiday debauchery. Nothing but a taut, condensing expanse. It embalmed the town, submerged it in transparent sap, as if it were to remain that way forever as a marvel of nature or an educational demonstration of what happens when time is utterly wasted. The only exception was a black mongrel with a tucked-in tail trotting along, blithely unaware it was Sunday. It dragged its shadow along behind it, and both vanished down Kościuszki as quickly as they had appeared.

I sensed that my accidental presence here was a scandal, that it played havoc with the established order of things, just as my body was disturbing the space, which swelled with self-sufficiency, and from which everyone hid in their homes, because otherwise they'd be distended and torn apart along with it, because Sunday had taken away their feeling of being needed, their bustle, the simple sequence of cause and effect. You only have to leave a place for seeds of madness to sprout there instantly, and a place like the Dukla market square becomes just like the human soul. A void takes over both the one and the other in exactly the same way, and at such a moment thoughts and walls crumble under their own weight. It was for that reason I went immediately to the bar at the tourist office. In there it always smelled of men, stale smoke, and beer. The tables had been cleared. They gleamed darkly, waiting for the evening. I ordered a Leżajsk and sat by the lilac-colored wall on which someone had painted yellow-green rushes and a silvery stretch of water. The barmaid said no more than "Two twenty" and disappeared into the back room. I peeked out of the half-open window. The lace curtain stirred in the breeze, revealing a part of the market square then immediately covering it again. The place was empty, quiet, cool. I was waiting for someone to emerge onto the sun-drenched square, the way you sometimes wait for a passerby who'll go ahead of you and cross the path of a black cat that just ran over the sidewalk.

Nothing but events, then. Yet some of them proliferate in the body like insistent thoughts, with time taking on an almost material form. They crystallize, precipitate, like salt. Subtle entities, among which we should include both thoughts and the images that memory has preserved, enter into unpredictable relations with one another, and the nature of these relations may never be fathomed. Because what real things could possibly link Dukla with that village from twenty-odd years ago, aside from the letter *u* that both have in their name.

That summer, in the village they started holding dances in the open air. It must have been a Saturday. A greenish gloom prevailed around the small square surfaced with paving stones. From time to time a traveling cinema showed movies here. Moths would gyrate in the stream of light from the projector and cast immense shadows onto the screen; the shadows were then fully entitled to take part in the action, because the films were usually black and white. But now a dance was in full swing. The teenagers stood where the shadows began. There were flashes of cheap church-fair belt buckles bearing bull's heads, colts, or mustangs. Large colored combs—the status symbol of the early seventies—poked out of the back pockets of jeans. Heat rose from the cement dance floor. We drew it into our nostrils and shuddered. Men put their arms around women in garish bouclé blouses, and the mixed smell of river air, sweat, perfume, and hot weather radiated like ripples on water, sweeping over us and engulfing us; at times I found it hard to breathe. The Tonette tape recorder, hooked up to an amplifier, was probably playing something by Anna Jantar or Irena Jarocka, while we circled the margins of the brightness like wild animals around a distant campfire, and like wild animals we understood nothing of the language of gestures, the pantomime of desire, resistance, acquiescence, and clandestine arrangements. But the smell needed no understanding. It entered into us; it filled our blood and our brains, in which there arose no questions, only an acrid, compelling amazement that was equally like shame and like rapture.

The yellow, orange, and willow-green blouses gave the women's breasts a provocative, rounded shape. And then there were hip-hugging bell-bottom pants made by the cunning tailors of Sokołów and Węgrów. Seams strained over the massive buttocks of the sons of country folk. And Beatles-style shoes with upturned tips, on stacked heels, with gold eyes in the lace-holes. And wrinkle-free shirts, and original Rifle jeans washed so often they were white—a sign that someone had relatives in America.

From thirty yards away the open-air dance hall looked like a golden grotto dug out of the blue-green shadows. It was a little as though the night had cracked open in this place and revealed its mysterious, warm interior, from which there issued a heady, overwhelming scent that was utterly unlike the smell of the world. Cold, sweetish wafts of air from the fields of still-green wheat, the musky odor of stables, the banal and vulgar aromas of jasmine and flowering lindens—these were the traces of workaday sedateness. Whereas there, in that hollow carved out of the dark, there was a purified atmosphere capable of turning the everyday inside out, revealing a side of it that was bloodshot, raw, terrifying.

The girls were unsightly. Seventeen and eighteen years old, their gold teeth glinting. Dumpy, with short legs and big breasts and backsides, they constituted faithful images of their destinies. Their light summer shoes revealed hard, callused heels. The guys with their sideburns looked like lovers from porno films. They danced ever closer and tighter, till in the end the dancing was so close it was no longer necessary, and they disappeared into the darkness.

Firefighters in civilian clothes would pack up the equipment and lock it back up in the firehouse, and that was that. A chill would blow in from the river and everything settled down again.

One Saturday the summer vacationers had appeared. The village was slowly becoming a tourist spot. A few cabins, a woebegone hostel, a kiosk selling Wyszków beer in its special bottles. The locals were used to it, and nothing special was going on. The Tonette was playing "Seven Girls on the *Albatross.*" The guys hadn't gotten into the swing of things yet. They were standing huddled in groups, smoking Start cigarettes. A few girls were milling about in pairs. In the bushes there were flashes of light from wine bottles and signet rings. No one raised their voice. Laughter would burst out and quickly die down again. The out-of-towners were bolder. They'd go out onto the cement dance floor with their loose city swagger, seemingly at ease, yet tense and conscious of the looks outsiders always attract. You could tell them by what they wore. Shorts, flip-flops, tight T-shirts, sandals, caps with visors, cretonne, cotton; beach, unconstrained boobs. But nothing much was happening. The Laskowski number would come to an end, Popcorn or Locomotiv GT would come on, and the young bucks, starting to feel bolder, would toss their bottles and cigarette butts aside, strut over to some girl or other and sweep her up in a dance that was awkward because it was still coy. So it began. From individual sparks.

Then, out of the dark came the girl, and mingled with the dancers. She wasn't from the village. She wasn't with any of the out-of-towners. She danced alone, though she must have known some of the vacationers, because once in a while she'd greet someone with a raised hand or a smile. She was wearing a white thigh-length dress. Her dark curly hair tumbled down her back. She kept flicking it from her forehead with a toss of her head. The suntanned skin of her arms and legs soaked up the light and became even darker, at the same time giving off a strange glow, as if inside her some process had transformed the wan electric glimmer into a magnetic, corporeal luster. The other dancing women looked like powdered corpses. She glided among them dexterously and indifferently and when she found herself a little room she'd spin around once or twice, and her whirling dress would ride up. Then she'd go back to tranquilly swinging her hips and arms. Her hands rose and fell softly as if she was exploring the lines of her own body in space, or yielding to a solitary caress. A gold cross winked on her low neckline.

Before I realized what I was doing, I found myself circling the dance floor in a sleepy, unthinking way, so as not to lose sight of her for a second; this wasn't at all necessary, as she stood out from the crowd, not because of her height but in her intense, sensual mobility. Her gestures possessed the deliberate inertia of matter. She resembled liquid mercury. Animals behave the same way, indifferent as to whether they're being watched. She was dancing barefoot. I stared at her feet. My eyes naturally, inevitably climbed her visibly muscular calves and her thighs, and while I had to imagine the rest, having no paradigm to work from, I was certain my imagination was fully accurate, that it was close to perfect. The little shadows in the hollows behind her knees were almost black. Over the loud music I could hear the slap of her feet against the cement surface. I could sense their hot, soft touch, but fear and shyness led my imagination to form an in-between image of a caress between her skin and the unfeeling ground. It was the same with the air. I could see it brushing against her arms and parting like smoke, while successive layers of it retained her touch, the moistness of her perspiration, her smell, and then vanished into the darkness; more and more layers came, but she had so much of it all she could fill the entire night, the entire atmosphere, and still remain the same, unscathed, animated and indifferent, as if she'd simply dried herself with a towel after taking a bath.

I tried to see her face, but the dark cloud of her ringlets veiled it or concealed it in disorderly shadow. From time to time I glimpsed white teeth or lowered eyelids. These detached, split-second images created a picture in harmony with the rest of her figure. She was beautiful with the kind of animal-like allure that seems to have no awareness of itself, and even if it does, it's conscious more of its own strength than of its beauty. She had a low forehead, sleepy almond-shaped eyes, broad cheekbones, and full lips that expressed a disquieting combination of disdain and sadness. All this, though, I saw later. That evening I only knew that her face must be as exquisite as her body. Among the farmers' daughters this barefoot vagabond looked like the child of kings. And as I crept around with dry throat and moist palms—as I snuck behind the backs of the onlookers to catch sight of her high breasts and the moment when her white dress would spin about her hips to reveal a firm thigh and the perfect oval hem of snow-white panties against a brown buttock—as I waited for her to raise her bare arm so I could glimpse the deep shadow beneath—eventually the image became so close that I felt myself entering into her body, not in the banal, sexual sense, but literally slipping into her taut brown skin; my hands filled her arms all the way to the fingertips, which I wiggled as if putting on gloves, and my face moved in the warmth of her smooth insides and became her face, and eventually my tongue became the inside of her tongue, and the same happened with everything else, with the red kingdom of tendons and muscles and the white strips of fat, and in the end she was entirely pulled over me, and I was wearing her to the furthest recesses of fingernails and hair. Her tight, languid body was the materialization of an oppressive aura that had haunted me that summer. All the scents, all the aromas, all the ethereal signs, all the emanations I'd discovered in that airy dance hall suddenly converged, clustered together, and like a genie in a bottle took refuge in her flesh, just as if she'd sucked them in through one of her crevices, drawn them inside through her belly button or her backside and in a single moment the world had become flat, distinct, and devoid of meaning.

I was thirteen years old and it all went to my head. The sun never set that summer. It stood permanently at its zenith, and our shadows were so paltry they called reality itself into question. Everything around shriveled up in the merciless light. The landscape flaked like old paint, things appeared from beneath other things and were no more realistic. I wandered through all the places I might find her. The painted plywood cabins became discolored in the swelter. It was a poor man's resort. Blue, yellow, red huts with two bunks and a communal toilet in the middle of a dusty field where the true maniacs did their best to play volleyball, tying wet cloths around their heads. I tried to track her down. I would sit under the tin awning of the cafeteria and drink greenish orangeade. The bottles bore no labels. The orangeade was over-carbonated, and sometimes it would explode. One day I spotted her going into a red cabin and closing the door behind her. I lingered for five more minutes, finishing off the warm pisswater as if it were chilled champagne, then I went there. The place was quiet. On the minuscule porch there was an empty Mistella wine bottle and nothing else. A thick curtain blocked the window. My legs trembled. Inside there was only darkness. Not a sound. I imagined a thousand things. I went up to the window, then lost my courage. I bought another orangeade and waited, but nothing happened.

July hung over the village like a sheet of blue metal. The river stank of silt. I hunted for where she was like a purblind cat. Every scrap of moving white brought the blood rushing to my head. I was sweaty, unclean, sticky from endless lemonades.

One day I was on the landing stage where boats and canoes were moored. I was spitting into the water. The white islets of spittle floated downstream. I watched them go. Then she appeared behind where I was sitting. She passed the landing stage and walked on. With her was a skinny female in a bathing suit. They trudged across the dull-colored beach. The skinny one's feet sank in up to the ankles, but the other girl strayed closer to the water, and at one point she left a clear footprint in the smooth wet sand. A moment later they turned toward the steps leading up to the hostel. I watched her climb higher and higher, her brown thighs moving beneath the parasol of her dress. Finally she paused at the very top, completely black against the blue sky, then disappeared. The whole thing lasted no more than half a minute, but I had awoken from an interminably long sleep. A boat with an outboard motor was coming up the river. The waves it made passed beneath the landing stage, lapped against the shore, and almost reached the footprint. My heart stopped. But the tongue of water was too short and the print remained untouched. I wanted to go there, but I wasn't alone. A kid from the village was sitting next to me; he was smoking a cigarette wrapped in his closed palm, and from time to time he'd offer me a drag. He was talking, but I didn't hear a thing. I was staring at the indentation in the sand. She was still present there. I knew her heat had remained in that place, her scent had remained, that the weight of her body had condensed there, filling the fragile shape, and only a few steps were needed for me to possess that solidified presence. The footprint was distinct. I could see the heel and the oval depressions of the toes. I cursed my buddy. He was sitting there prattling on in a singsong accent that was as languorous as the heat-benumbed river.

Then a noisy family came along with an inflatable mattress, blankets, and a host of children in red polka-dot bathing suits. They spread out across the spot and lay down, exposing their white bellies to the sun.

When we left there half an hour later, I held back for a moment and picked up a handful of sand from the trampled place. My eyes hurt. The whole time I kept staring at the nonexistent, desecrated footprint, so as not to lose it. I poured a little sand into my pocket. We went off in search of shade.

When the sky terrifies us with its emptiness we go looking for signs upon the earth. That was what I was thinking to myself as I sat and waited for someone to appear on the market square. But the only thing there was the town hall with its white walls, though on mild winter afternoons the whiteness had a blue sheen like air behind a windowpane. By the entrance the light blue cranium of a public telephone hung on the wall, while inside, instead of municipal offices, they'd built a gym so the young guys would have a choice, so instead of always having to go to the Gumisia or the Graniczna right away, they could go there later. Now it was all closed up, there was nothing but imperceptibly lengthening shadows.

I sipped my Leżajsk and began to grasp the fact that the Sunday emptiness comes from the silence and the absence of distinct smells. The wind had swept them all away, and besides, stone-built towns don't have a clear scent. Changes in stone happen so slowly that if there is decay, it takes place beyond the reach of the senses. It takes too long, it's hard to comprehend, because it occurs in a nonhuman space. Rather like the kinds of sound we can't hear, yet which cause us to die. From the back room came the disco song "Polka-Dot Panties," along with the clatter of dishes and a faint whiff of coffee. It was almost visible in the air: golden brown, floating in front of the lilac-colored wall, interwoven with the grayish smoke from my cigarette. A moment later it was smothered by the stench of stale ash, sweat, and the outbreath of countless drunken conversations.

The afternoon had gradually blurred the outlines of the town hall, and in its place there appeared a manor house encircled by a goodly wooden Fence that yet requyred repair in places. In said Manor a Dining Room, entry to the which was gayned by a Door upon iron hinges, with handle and latch likewise of iron. By said door, a walled Fireplace, a green Stove of poor quality, upon the one side and the other a black carpenter-bilt Cupboard, in the which two grated doors on high, while below two further, upon iron hinges. One folding Table of goodly dimensions. Three Windows, lead-cased, upon the which two wooden shutters. Adjoining said room, two Bedchambers. Second room for womenfolk. Beyond, a Chamber containing one door. Subjoining this room, a small Chamber without door; beyond that a further chamber. Small Alcove to side, opposite said dining room, with entrance door, in it a whyte Stove of plain tile, lindenwood table, one great window with lead casing. Between room and alcove, two small Chambers, with slyding doors. Small Room by entrance hall, with door. Entrance hall of goodly size, reached by large doorway, with lock, and iron holdfast on upper part. From said entrance hall a Kitchen, off kitchen small chamber for kitchenwares, with slyding door. To side of kitchen, Pantry. In pantry, one window with wooden casing. Entyre manor shingle-roofed, in places shingles requyre repair. Two stables, one carridge house, also shingle-roofed. Third stable empty. Beneath manor, 4 vaulted sellars. Entrance to manor from town via large timber Gate, with iron holdfast and two iron fastenings mounted upon the gateposts . . .

That was how things were three hundred years ago behind the window that back then did not exist. Iron, wood, sooty stoves, rotting shingles, smoke, fug, the semidarkness of overcast days, low ceilings, damp, mice, walls permeated with smells, and doors, endless doors to new rooms, chambers, alcoves, hallways, cupboards, dressers, chests, closets, in which the dust, the cobwebs, and the stale air were subjected to the action of time, its monotonous currents, that leave a residue upon the surface of objects. All this is so very reminiscent of memory, with its unpredictable structure, and uncountable number of places in which everything can start up one more time from the beginning, like some insane inventory, a list of things and possibilities, down to the furthest depths, and there's no final depth anyway, because a deeper one will always open up, and another, because the slightest moment can be divided into even smaller ones, and those smaller ones burst like fireworks into hundreds of stars, each with a different color and taste and shape, and so on and on, till the mind itself explodes, and that's the only infinity we have, the rest is merely its fragments raised to the umpteenth power and rendered immobile, and thus dead.

At last something started to happen. People came in. Only two of them, but it was enough. I got up and left the bar, trying to find the tunnel, the passageway, via which they'd brought their bodies through the afternoon.

The bells of Mary Magdalene had sprung into motion. I had a desire to go there. I was drawn to Maria Amalia, but it occurred to me that this was the hour of the old women, and I wouldn't be alone in the church. I was drawn to the small figure in the furbelowed gown. This was a death that smelled of rice powder, angel's water, and languid swoons. This could have been what Bernini's St. Teresa looked like once her ecstasy had run its course. The sound of the bells drifted over the town. The ponderous metallic wave spread in concentric circles, separating the sky from the earth. People leaked from their houses drop by drop, rolled from entranceways like ponderous balls, stood blinded by the brightness of the market square, made decisions or circled the square, driven by inertia, then gathered in small groups smoking, brushing specks of dust off their clothing and discussing what to do for the rest of the day. Vespers was beginning in Dukla. At Mary Magdalene, at the Cistercian monastery, at the Gumisia and in the Krist-Bar, and at the Graniczna.

My bus was waiting at the station. We set off toward Żmigród. The driver left the door open. There were no other passengers, it was just him and me.

The radio was on. After we drove through Iwla things returned to where they belonged. I couldn't be bothered to wonder what was hidden in the houses along the road. They stood there in a row, pressed up flat against the landscape, with no room for either thoughts or mice to creep in. Dukla faded with every stop. It lost its clarity, like a dream after you wake up, a dream that leaves only an outline, a gray mark against a drab background.

That's why I keep returning to this story from over twenty years ago. I'm convinced it's composed of the same basic elements that the vortex of time arranges in different constellations, but whose nature remains unchanged, the way that water, salt, and metals form into various kinds of bodies so as to save us from boredom. Dukla was made of the same atoms, and so was that summer, when I went sniffing along her trail in the heat with a handful of sand in the pocket of my Odra jeans, and the sand diminished as the quartz rubbed through the cotton, disappearing or turning into an intangible dust.

From time to time I'd slip my hand in, take out a few grains, and taste them. I'd leave them on my tongue, press them against the roof of my mouth, and in the end my saliva would wash the particles away.

I'd swing by the beach. People were lying on the shore as if the waves had thrown them there. There was a smell of singed fat. Every so often they entered the water and thrashed about like fish on a hook. There was no intermediate state—either immobility or hysteria. But she wasn't there.

It was as though the brown color of her flesh didn't depend on the sun, as if she'd been born that way, or she could absorb the light of the moon by night. I roamed among the bare bodies, fully dressed like some kind of bashful pervert. The breasts, buttocks, thighs of the other women made no more of an impression on me than my little sister's dolls. There was something ludicrous about those lifelessly toiling bodies. They lay there like stuck-out tongues, gasping for breath. I was thirteen years old and I couldn't understand voluntary motionlessness. I would climb the steep stairs, nose around among the shacks, circle her cabin. It always looked the same. Open window, thick curtains, and a silence so profound it could have hidden anything. The pink walls took on an almost black hue in the glare of the day. They were so distinct, so separate from the world and so terrifyingly real, it was as if they were made of some substance so dense it absorbed the sunlight to the very last drop. Darkness so very evident is only ever found in dreams, or immediately after an attack of sunstroke. I'd be rescued by the tin roof of the cafeteria, a bottle of orangeade, and the fear of being unmasked. I would walk away, trail through the dust of the deserted village, and usually end up at the Ruch Club, where it was always cool and the dark smell of cinnamon cookies hung in the air. The turned-off television would be waiting for the evening, the server in her white apron sat with her elbows on the countertop, staring into her daydreams. In the gloom of the place she looked so lonely that despite myself I felt I could trust her, sensing we were linked by something rooted in boundless melancholy. I took my fruit juice and drank it at a metal table, repeating the gestures and grimaces I'd observed men making when they would disgustedly take a mouthful of bitter beer.

I performed my dour ritual every day, but in vain. I was convinced she'd left. Gone. All the same I kept returning to the old places. Sadness stupefies even more than hope.

Then, one afternoon something white moved on the porch of her cabin. True, it wasn't actually her, but it was her white dress. It was hanging on a line strung between the pillars. There was a gentle breeze. Next to the dress hung a pair of white panties stuck up with two clothespins. A gust of wind lifted them in my direction. It was blowing diagonally from upriver, in other words from the east. I was entranced by the sight. I forgot where I was. The white cotton—rounded, filled-out, taut—recreated the shape of her body. The sweltering, unseen afternoon had slipped into her underwear so as to play havoc with my imagination. It was then I understood that she was as vast as the day is long, as all the air, all the world, that she had no end and no beginning, that she was surrounding me on all sides, that I was in her, that this white scrap of fabric was merely a sign of her all-embracing presence, a signal for a blind man, a concession to the imperfection of the senses. I felt the soft, warm touch of her bronzed skin. Because if she could be so great that she was invisible, it meant her thigh or her knee could reach all the way here, those few yards. I half closed my eyes and in the middle of that trash-strewn, godforsaken place I surrendered to the caress. My ears and cheeks burned. I rubbed against myself like a cat. Her condensed, elusive presence was so palpable it obscured reality. The gust of air that had passed through her panties formed into a living, pulsing body. I think I moved forward, took a step or two in that direction, imagining the objects around me—the brightly painted cabins, the flag over the beach, the tops of the trees, and all the rest—to be a dream or an illusion.

Suddenly the door to the porch opened and her skinny girlfriend from the beach came out. She was wearing the same bathing suit. She gave me a hostile look and snapped: "What do you want?" She took in the laundry. As she disappeared back into the cabin she gave me a last unfriendly glance over her shoulder.

At that time I made no attempt to work out the relationship between the two women. It seemed natural that beauty should be found in the company of ugliness. Her girlfriend had a pale, wan face and short mousy hair. She looked like a young boy who'd grown old before he'd reached adulthood. Her pallid, bony body moved without an ounce of grace, as if it was overcoming exhaustion or the resistance of its own sinews by sheer effort of will. I'd seen her at the cafeteria buying something to drink, or with her basket at the store in the village. She walked quickly. She wore shabby clogs that twisted painfully on the cobblestones. She kept her head down as she passed people. She never spoke with anyone. One time, in the store a half-drunk guy started talking to her. She left immediately. I think it was her who had washed the other one's clothes.

Time died away between Saturdays. It lost its light, transparent quality. It swelled, thickened, became inert, stuck to the body, and my life came to resemble a march into the wind. I felt like I was trying to run in water up to my chest. My gestures trailed behind me long after I'd made them. I was convinced they left traces in the air. Because back then time was very much like air. Or water. On Saturday evenings, though, it regained its rightful form. It flowed so quickly that it got ahead of me. I could see it fleeing, the way landscapes slip away from the window of a train. Nothing could be done. In theory they remain where they are, but you have the feeling that it's the landscapes leaving us behind, not the other way around.

She came to every dance. For a month. Always alone. Her companion must have stayed in the cabin, though there was no light to be seen in the window. She sat in the dark, glowing phosphorically like an old skeleton. That must have been enough for her. In the meantime, her friend was gyrating amid the other dancers, animated, impetuous, and taut in her magnificent integument, as if she were about to burst, explode, from an excess of her own existence. The eyes of the farm boys followed her as though attached by strings, but none of them was brave enough. She guessed their thoughts, and once in a while she would assail one or another of them. She'd lean back slightly, push out her chest, and they'd be left dumbstruck, treading on their own shoelaces, enclosed in a whirl of air she had set in motion, while she was already elsewhere, engrossed in herself, guiltless and absent.

Older folks came to the dances too. Women in particular. They brought with them the barn-dance custom of sitting on benches around the walls and, as they swallowed the dust, sharpening their tongues or simply watching without a word, sinking into their own past life like a vivid dream with eyes wide open. Here there was no dust and no walls, but there were a few benches around the dance floor. There they sat, fifty or sixty years old, in green and brown and black head scarves that in the darkness resembled hoods. As they talked, their gold teeth flashed like lit matches. They looked like jurors in a courtroom. In twos and threes, their heads leaning in to one another, they examined the throng and muttered among themselves, not letting the spinning couples out of their sight for a second.

As usual I dodged about, following her white dress. I orbited the hubbub of the dance, lurking at its edges, intent and at the same time hopelessly vulnerable, my secret inscribed on my face. She would be turning tight circles in the middle of the dance floor, widening them then once again shrinking to the irreducible shape of her own outline; but even when she was virtually standing in place, restricted, hemmed in by the crowd, she kept dancing, she danced without moving, but she was just as impetuous, because her presence alone was a scandal and a provocation. Perhaps the blood surged so intensely through her body that its pulse was visible. All at once, in one of those moments of stillness as the singer Irena Jarocka was taking a breath, in the split second of half-quiet I heard the voice of an old woman from a nearby bench. She said, "Whore," then the music started up again, drawing the hundreds of dancers into its circulation.

The girl couldn't have heard it. No one did aside from me. Everything was taking its regular course. Some people were moving off toward the bushes.

They would come back unsteadier on their feet, or with their clothes in greater disarray, or they wouldn't come back at all, and it would only be the morning dew that woke them in a haystack, which in those parts was known as a *mendel*, the old measure of fifteen, because each stack was made of fifteen sheaves of hay. So everything was the way it always was. "Yellow Autumn Leaf," a slow number, offered a chance to catch your breath and whisper blandishments. "She gave me it without a word / And yet I knew full well." Some of the guys wore flares decorated with gold studs and close-fitting shirts patterned with vertical zigzags in all the colors of the rainbow. The coolest girls were in tight cotton pants that were cream-colored with a fine brown check. What else? I guess big colorful East German Ruhl watches on wrists, and huge bright plastic signet rings in the shape of cut stones: purple, yellow, green, or white. Around their necks they had rectangular wooden pendants that bore an enameled photo of ABBA, strung on a thin cord. Slade too, I think. There were masses of such things at church fair stalls in August and you could take your pick, so there must have been other heroes too. Yes, there was Hoss, Ben, the other Cartwrights from *Bonanza*. So nothing special was going on. The world abided in its established fluctuating form and beer couldn't have cost more than four zlotys, while Start cigarettes in the rough orange-colored soft packs were 5.50, but something like a fissure in existence had opened up in front of me, something like an alluring wound in the skin of the everyday. I didn't yet know how to translate that word into the language of reality. But I did know its taste: acrid, dark, intense, and bitter, like things that despite ourselves we're unable to resist, and in fact do not wish to. The word, spoken in a harsh lifeless voice, unfolded in the air and wrapped her figure in an aura. Now she was dancing in the glow of her own body and the glow of the imprecation.

I was thirteen years old and there was much I didn't understand. All I sensed was that in a single moment my love had ceased to be an innocent and embarrassing game, and had become something forbidden. I was thirteen years old and I could feel that beauty always involved peril, that in essence it was a form of evil, a form that we may desire as if we were desiring good.

Now, passing through Żmigród, I can see this very clearly. The bus picks up one tipsy passenger, stops at the little town square then heads downhill, turning left by Leśko's dairy and moving along the strange road that neatly separates the hills on the left from the level terrain on the right. But back then everything was simply a play of shadows, smells, sounds. A bizarre arrangement of the physical manifestations of the world, which formed themselves into a momentary passageway, a channel that led to the other side of time and landscape. This flip side of the visible was essentially identical to its regular face, except it was infinitely more attractive because it was unaffected by gravity and completely given over to the laws of the imagination. This one word coming into contact with her body had turned inside out, become its own opposite, so as once and for all to shake my faith in unambiguity.

One time I went to Dukla in the winter. It was January, though it was more like a snowy November or a permanent dusk. Sky and earth were merged. The sprawling outskirts of Jasło, the hangarlike warehouses, jagged rows of snow fences, indeterminate outlines of people twenty yards from the roadway, houses with motionless smoke issuing from their chimneys, and all the other familiar things—everything only half existed. A memory of archetypes was needed to uncover its true meaning and purpose. "This is a house. This is a dog. This is Jane's cat." The mist-flattened contours barely revealed themselves. Everything except what was definitively black belonged to this half-snowy, half-watery state of convergence. It was a color-blind dream, or an old dying television set. Even the black—the vertical strokes of trees, the horizontal lines of balustrades on the footbridges—even these things looked more like their own shadows. It was as if the objects themselves had vanished, leaving only their faint impressions in a suspension of gray light. On top of everything it so happened that I'd not slept the previous night and had greeted the day on my feet. I'd not crossed the boundary of waking. Unreality had taken hold of that Tuesday and wouldn't let go. Right at the beginning, in Gorlice, at seven in the morning, when I'd been buying a Red Bull for the road, the guy in front of me in line was wearing classic wide 1970s pants with a pressed seam and a so-called "cool jacket," nylon, all black but with cornflower-blue sleeves, in other words early Gierek, Różyckiego bazaar in Warsaw, with a broad plastic zipper. He stood there shivering, though it was warm in the store. Then, when his turn came he said: "One from the fridge, please, one of those with the penguin." He left the store, shuffling with the familiar step of someone whose foot doesn't entirely believe that when it rises from the ground, the ground is going to wait for it to return.

Before I got on the bus I'd met Mr. Marek, who as usual told me the story about how he'd once been rich and had bought dinner for someone or other. As usual I gave Mr. Marek something toward his ticket, and as usual he headed straight for the store.

But now I was passing through Jasło already. Under the bridge the Wisłok looked like a blacktop highway. Nothing was reflected in it. The bus was long and comfortable. It rocked and hummed, and up front a TV monitor hanging from the roof was showing a furiously colorful movie, probably from California, because there were palm trees, swimming pools, stretch limos, naked women, and blood was flowing. The screen looked like a window onto the truer side of the world. Around me, all the way to the horizon everything was dull and indistinct, while up there was a bright rectangle of heavenly colors and people devoting themselves to wealth, love, and death. The fellow sitting next to me took off his cap with earflaps and stared, now at the screen, now out the window. Both views must have bored him, because in the end he crossed his arms on his belly and fell asleep.

In Krosno, water was dripping from the rooftops. The ingeniously wrought roofs of Krosno are designed for thaws and rain. The water eddies, gurgles, meanders, and drips in those miraculous products of the roofer's art as if they were some kind of meteorological carillon, till in the end they find their gutter and trickle down to the street; there, old folks walk timidly along, their elbows raised like the wings of startled chickens, because warmth has reached the rooftops but down below, on the sidewalk, it's still freezing, and glassy tongues protrude from the jaws of the drainpipes. That was how it was. I was catching my balance, I had a good hour till my connecting bus to Barwinek. Mist, water, and the alienation of sleeplessness, when even in a clean shirt and with money in his pocket a guy feels like an old wino.

I tried saving myself by having a beer with a large shot of cassis in it, but it was just as indistinct as everything else. Haziness was seeping into everything both alive and dead. I thought to myself that before I got there Dukla would disappear, evaporate into the air like an old memory. I wanted to buy Mr. Michalak's guide, *Dukla and Surroundings*. I'd seen it in a shop window one time in Dukla, but it had been a Sunday and the store was closed. Now I went looking for it in Krosno. I entered the bookstore on the street that swings to the right beyond the bridge and wraps around the base of the old town. Inside it was quiet and warm. A priest was conferring in an undertone with the young woman behind the counter. Radio Maryja was playing in one corner. There was a smell of turpentine and printed matter. The books were arranged on shelves around the walls. Most of them were about holiness and miracles, but there were also items about the Masons, the Mormons, Manson, and the worldwide conspiracy. There wasn't anything about Dukla. I tried to eavesdrop on the conversation between the priest and the clerk, but they were whispering softly, conspiratorially, their heads together.

I couldn't see the priest's face. Radio Maryja was playing its favorite song, with a catchy harmonica melody and a mixed choir singing about how victory would come to the white eagle and the Polish race. Dressed in black and leaning forward, the priest looked a little like a conspirator. He left the store at a smart pace, I saw him toss a bundle of books into an old Opel and drive off. The young woman's perfume wafted around the place. The air had been disturbed by the cleric and had drawn the scent toward the door. The clerk wore glasses. Or at least she should have.

After that there was the immensity of the Krosno bus station. The tarmac was vast as an airport, tiny beat-up old buses with signs saying Krempna, Wisłoczek, Zyndranowa were waiting where there should have been jet liners taking off. My bus was right near the end; it was yellow and so very helpless you had the urge to take it in your fingers, lead it out onto the roadway, give it a gentle push, and say: Come on little one, don't be afraid, off you go.

I wasn't mistaken. Dukla was in danger of ceasing to exist. As usual I took the alley between Mr. Szczurek's photography studio and the display cabinet of Mr. Kogut, doctor of veterinary science. The town hall could barely be seen against the sky. It looked like a piece of the latter that had been cut out with scissors and had slipped down a little ways and come to rest on the pavement. A two-dimensional stage decoration with little cardboard doors at the top. The air pressure was plummeting, but the air itself remained still. The warm southern *halny* wind hadn't yet begun to blow. Right now it was probably gathering strength over the Great Hungarian Plain, stretching out its paw and feeling the south side of the Carpathians for fissures, low-lying passes, and broader saddles by which it could break through and descend on the unsuspecting Podgórze region, sowing mental havoc in its inhabitants. Just in case, then, I stepped into the bar at the tourist office.

There were three guys at a table, wordlessly drinking vodka. They were simply raising their glasses to their lips and tipping them. They paid no attention to each other.

Before the *halny* blows, everything is quiet and alien. Sparks dance inside bodies, nerves grow taut and overheated, the skin stops protecting them and for this reason the boundary between everyday banality and madness grows slender as a single hair. People stop being able to distinguish between themselves and the world and mistake themselves for reality, whereas in fact it's only that the mind is weakening, and instead of arranging the chaos around itself into some semblance of meaning, it thinks only about itself.

The guys were just regular guys, drab and unshaven. They didn't even look at me, but they sensed my presence like that of an unwelcome animal. A wet trail on the floor led to their table. Each of them was tapping out his own rhythm with his foot. A white sneaker, a tall zip-up black boot, and the tip of something that could have been an overshoe or a lined rubber boot. A clattering sound came from the back room. I knocked on the counter with my two-zloty coin. I had no desire to linger there. The barmaid came through, poured my drink as if I were transparent, and swept the money into the drawer without looking. I drank up and left so quickly I didn't even taste the beer till I reached the vaulted gateway that leads from the market square into a small courtyard where in the summertime there's a table and three chairs under a tree.

There was still no wind. It's always that way before the *halny*, like taking air into your lungs and trying to live with it for as long as possible. On the corner of Kościuszki a woman hurled something at the feet of a man in a green jacket and stomped off. The man picked the thing up, started to straighten it, push it out, fold it, then ran after her. To this day I don't know what it was. It was brown. I walked over, but there was no trace on the sidewalk. The couple that had been arguing had already vanished into the Graniczna. There was nothing to hold on to. The mind and the gaze moved in every direction without encountering any obstacle. Matter and memory yielded before them and wherever you looked, whatever you thought about, there was nothing but the void of geography all the way to the borders of Krosno province, or the amorphous deep waters of all that had gone before, including even the birth waters. That's how things look moments before the *halny* begins. Weightlessness, emptiness, and the slackening of the mind, you have the feeling of having swallowed the whole world, and there's a hollow echo in your belly. Nothing but the misery of isobars, forms of existence swelling and overlapping, and transcendence getting in the way of immanence. At these moments the imagined mingles with the real and the mountain-dwelling Górals of Podhale clutch their temples in despair, blood is spilled in the Pod Cyckiem bar, and don't even try to separate the guys doing the fighting. Suicides go looking for quiet spots to hang themselves, love turns to rape, and vodka consumed gathers in the organism without appearing to cause any harm; you sit up straight, stiff and bored, till in the end the brain explodes like magnesium and in the white light of madness the improbable becomes the ordinary. Snow slides from the shingles and the roof ridges glisten like blades. That's how things should be.

So I decided to try and find the house that R. and I had discovered when we were here in the summer. At that time dusk had been falling. We walked down Cergowska, turned into Podwale, then into Zielona. It was an inconspicuous cottage of blackened wood. It stood at the far end of an untended yard. A yellow light shone in the window. Five minutes later and everything would have been completely dark, but the remains of the daylight allowed us to take a look at this yard or lot. It was laid out in a truly curious order. Scraps, pieces, and torn lengths of rusty sheet metal had been arranged in a tidy geometrical pile. Someone had gone to a lot of trouble to organize the misshapen pieces into an almost perfect cuboid. Elsewhere, rocks, rubble, and brick fragments lay in a pyramidal prism smoothed into an exact cone. Shards and pebbles had been stuck in the crevices between the larger pieces as precisely as a mason would have done. Whole and half bricks had been ordered in a neat hexagonal stack. In another place, leftover roofing paper and plastic sheeting had been gathered together, rolled up and aligned according to type and size. The tubes and rolls had been placed so neatly upon one another in a tapering pile that on the top there was one roll crowning the whole. Wood too had been sorted according to size and shape. Rotten planks in one place, short lengths of thick beams elsewhere in a cubic mound, like building blocks. Next to them lay scrap iron. A snarl of rusted shapes had been disentangled. To one side pipes, rods, rails, channel bars, in other words long thin objects; to another small irregular polyhedrons, old bicycle parts, kitchen fittings, tin cans, and God knows what all else. These items, whose shape prevented them from matching one another, had been tipped together to form a rounded semicircular heap, care being taken to make sure nothing jutted out to spoil the relatively even outline. Beneath the overhang of a shed built of sawmill offcuts, glass had been collected. Hundreds, maybe even thousands of bottles had been stacked on one another to form a wall of glass, necks toward the shed, bottoms facing out. Here too a rudimentary order had been maintained. Green, brown, and clear glass were each kept together, in addition to which the bottles had been grouped according to size and shape: flat ones were separate from round ones, while half-liter bottles were not mixed with quarter liters, or with one-liter cola or orangeade bottles. The scheme was exceedingly complex, since three colors and multiple shapes give a dizzying number of possible combinations. Then there were jars, also sorted according to their dimensions. A little farther still was an old tree with spreading branches, from which there hung loops of string, coils of electric cord, small and large lengths, and snippets, tied together, fastened tight, solid, dangling like horses' tails. There were also stuffed plastic bags, over a dozen colored sacks filled with who knew what, but certainly something light, because they swung in the breeze. It looked like the creation of the world. A path had been trodden through the heaps of trash. It looked as if the creator of this order strolled around his work, admiring it, straightening it up from time to time.

We went toward the ruins of the synagogue. Birch saplings had taken root in the top of a wall several feet above the ground. We could hear the rustle of young leaves. At this point R. said he really liked the place we'd seen, that the person in that wretched old shack, the worst house on a whole street of big, expensive, ugly houses, that that person was just trying to give meaning to his world, and that was fine, he wasn't trying to change it, just put it in order a little, the way you organize your thoughts, and often that's enough to stop you from going mad. That was what R. said, so I gave up on the idea of creation, because it seemed like R. was right.

So now I wanted to go back there to have something my eyes and my thoughts could fasten onto, something straightforward and self-evident, something that had been done for its own sake. And I did go, but there was snow in the yard and the piles were hidden under little white hillocks. They looked like something accidental and natural. There were no footsteps leading to the door, nor was smoke rising from the chimney. A handful of faded plastic bags hung from the leafless tree. They looked like dismal fruits. I think they were filled with other bags. The first gusts of the *halny* came from the south and rocked them. I quickly walked away. The bus from Barwinek smelled of the wind.

In the dictionary it says "dukla" means "a small mineshaft dug for exploratory purposes, in search of deposits, for ventilation, or as a primitive means of extracting ore."

That's right. My method is primitive. It's like drilling at random. In principle it could be done anywhere. It doesn't make much difference, since the world is round. Like memory, which begins from a single point, a dot, then spins in layers and turns ever widening circles, so as to swallow us up and bring about our ruin in utterly unneeded abundance. At that point we begin to turn around, retreat, pretend we've walked into all this accidentally, by mistake, that in fact someone's taken us for a ride, deceived us as if we were children, and now all we want to do is go to our mom, to hold onto her skirt and cry from shame and helplessness.

That summer, as always, July turned imperceptibly into August, and despite the relentless swelter a reminder that the vacation was passing could be smelled in the air. The cowpats in the meadows dried in the twinkling of an eye. You could flip them over with the toe of your shoe. Metallic green beetles halted in the sudden glare, then quickly sought shade. Dust hovered permanently over the roadway. The willows along the river smelled as if they were on fire. The water level had fallen and sandbars emerged in the middle of the stream. You could wade out to them in water that only came up to your chest. Then you could lie there on your back, feeling the tickle of the river and the coarse sand yielding beneath the weight of your body. Some people even crossed all the way to the other bank and stood there proudly, hands on their hips, then a moment later they'd be taken aback by the sight of their own village, which they'd never seen before from that angle. In the evening, trucks carrying metal barrels would drive down to the river. People were taking water for their livestock. The wells were beginning to dry up. Horses stood to their bellies in the water and drank.

That summer, for the first time I got so drunk I passed out. My pals dragged me to my uncle and aunt's house and left me there. I woke up at dawn. I was wet from the dew. A red sun was rising over the black line of pine and aspen thickets. There was no wind whatsoever, yet the poplars along the road were rustling as always.

The firefighters had called off the outside dances and taken their Tonette tape player back into the firehouse. The nights were cold now. One evening they threw a proper bash, indoors. There was a buffet with vodka and beer, and taped music was only played in the breaks when the accordion player and the guitarist and drummer were temporarily exhausted. Yellow dust swirled in the firehouse air. The dancers were drenched in sweat. Some time before midnight a police car pulled up and two uniforms came in to look for someone. They found him, but he got away. He even took a swing at one of the cops, I saw a cap with an eagle badge lying on the floor. The guy ran off into the darkness between the barns. The dogs barked after him. The other cop took out his gun and fired into the night. That summer was the first time I heard a real shot.

One day we were kicking a ball around on the volleyball court. In the end it rolled into some bushes and stayed there. Nothing was hanging on the porch of her cabin. Another empty Mistella bottle stood next to the first one. We dispersed lethargically in search of shade. We were tan and bored. We were thirsty. I didn't have a penny. I moved off toward the concrete bunker that housed the washrooms and showers. Inside was a cool semidarkness. Light seeped in through the narrow windows up by the ceiling and came to a halt there as if it lacked the strength to continue down. I took a drink, trembling from the chill. On the nearest faucet there was a bundled-up towel. At the far end was a hallway that led to the showers. From there came the noise of running water. At moments it sounded like a dry crackle. I splashed water on my face. The running water stopped and I heard someone call: "Kryśka! Hand me the towel!" Then a second later: "Kryśka!"

I picked it up. It was damp. I took it and walked toward the showers. The small rectangle of window at the end of the hallway was blindingly bright, though it didn't illuminate anything. The plastic curtain moved in the last stall. I didn't see it, I just heard the rustle. I walked with the towel held out in front of me. I came to a stop very close, and then the semitransparent hanging opened completely. When she took the towel she had to tug it slightly from my hand. What I'd seen was the merest outline of a figure, a dark silhouette against the golden glare. Her hair was almost straight now. It lay on her shoulders, heavy and wet. I thought to myself that I'd finally get a look at her face, but all I could see was light, streams of sunlight filtering through the dirty pane, then refracting around her head.

She said: "You've been following me around." She shifted slightly, and with her moved the warm, close air that was saturated with her scent, the metallic smell of water, and the aura of the wet wall. I was enveloped in a stifling, palpable cloud, and it was as if I'd found myself within her, as if I were touching her skin from inside. I could feel the springy, yielding integument of the world and I was afraid to move, because every gesture, every tremor returned to me in the form of an infinitely pleasurable, mortal caress. I was breathing deeply. The air stole through my veins. It was permeated with her being. She touched my cheek, her hand slipped down to my neck and I felt droplets of water trickling down my back. Then, somewhere far off we heard the lifeless clatter of clogs. She withdrew her hand. I turned and ran outside. Blinded by the sun, I didn't stop till I was in the middle of the village. An old woman was hanging a bucket on the fence. To the west, a small white cloud had drifted over the old cholera cemetery, but a moment later it was gone.

Dukla, then. It's a strange town, from which there's no longer anywhere to go. Farther on there's only Slovakia, and even farther the Bieszczady Mountains, but on the way you pass through the back of the proverbial beyond and nothing of any importance is going to happen, nothing, there are just frail houses squatting by the roadside like sparrows on a wire, and between them windswept pastures inevitably ending in a sky that rises then curves, hangs overhead, and comes to rest on the opposite rim of the horizon. That's right—Dukla as the overture to empty spaces. Where can anyone go from Dukla? From Dukla you can only return. It's the Hel Peninsula of the Carpathians, an Ultima Thule in the form of a town. Beyond here there's nothing but wooden Lemko cottages and the concrete remnants of Le Corbusier's bastards—which is to say, things that present no challenge to the landscape. There are never more than two buses waiting at the bus station at any one time. Long-haul trucks from Romania slow down for a moment, for half a mile, then at the Cistercian monastery they floor it again.

You drink a beer at the Graniczna, walk out onto the market square, and your imagination swells like a balloon in a physics lesson when it's put in the chamber of a vacuum pump. And at that moment Dukla becomes the center of the world, omphalos of the universe—the thing from which all things begin, the core around which are strung the successive layers of mobile events that are turned irreversibly into immobile fictions: One-horse *dorozhka* from Iwonicz 3 crowns, two-horse *dorozhka* 7 crowns, stagecoach one crown fifty. The stagecoach departs at 6:00 A.M., 7:30 A.M., and 2:00 P.M. One may spend the night at Lichtmann's inn for one crown fifty, and eat in Henryk the Musician's breakfast room. Three thousand inhabitants, of whom two and a half thousand are Jews. The year is, let's say, 1910. Taken together, the whole thing resembles a sepia photograph or an old celluloid film still—

the one and the other both burn easily and leave an empty space behind. It's as if time itself had been burned up. When things that exist in space go to ruin, they leave a vacuum that we fill with other things. And how is it with time? In all probability it fuses together like something organic and continues on its way, because we're accustomed to continuity, which is a little like immortality. And what if Baroness Mniszech, the Jews, and the *dorozhkas* left some space behind them, some unoccupied places, holes, like the ones left by cigarette burns in your best suit?

When I keep revisiting Dukla, then, I don't care about the stagecoaches, or the Jews, or any of that. I'm only interested in whether time is a disposable item like, say, a Povela Corner paper tissue from Tarnów. Only that.

Not long after that, she left. The cabin was locked up. The curtain was gone from the window—they must have brought it with them. The pane shone blackly. The empty bottles had vanished from the porch. The clothesline had disappeared. The resort was dying down. The green-painted plywood canoes had been dragged from the beach up to the shed where all summer long a guy with one pinned-up shirtsleeve had rented canoes and oars for two zlotys a time. The only thing left at the dock was a white laminated plastic boat tied up with a chain. We used to sit in it sometimes. The chain was a long one, but the current would nudge the boat toward the shore. We'd smoke there. Sometimes drink wine. I did it furtively. Now all I needed was the bitter taste and the warmth in my belly. A hundred yards downstream some wooden scows were moored.

Slightly older boys would go there and unbutton the girls' blouses. At dusk you could hear giggles. The water carried the sounds a long way. We'd listen in on their conversations. I didn't understand much of it. Next to the scows, on the shore there were big piles of opened mussel shells from the river. The other boys told me people used to feed mussels to the pigs.

One day very close to the end, to my departure, I went back there. Water was dripping from one of the faucets. I turned it off. I wanted everything to be completely quiet. All I could hear was the squeak of my rubber soles on the dry floor. I went into the last stall and closed the plastic shower curtain behind me. Just like before, the sun was shining through the narrow horizontal window. The cracked tiles gleamed like semitransparent gold. It looked as though something lay behind them, that another world began there. The place smelled of wet wall and of the sadness of somewhere where so many strangers had stood naked. It was a little like their reflections had frozen still and been abandoned here. Greasy water had pooled in the drain, with a white flake of soap and a clump of hair. A memento of everyone. The wooden platform was light gray and almost dry. No one had been by here in a long while. In the corner there was an empty yellow sachet of shampoo. I picked it up. Inside there was only air and a faint scent. I was afraid. Someone passed by on the other side of the wall and said something to another person. It didn't occur to me to take my clothes off and pretend I was taking a shower. Or rather it did, but the idea seemed too bold to me. I somehow didn't imagine a thirteen-year-old could go into someone else's shower, just like that. But I was even more scared by the thought that I could recreate her existence with my body. I stood in that pathetic cubic space and allowed myself only to touch. The tiling was cold and stuck to my fingers. The cracks and gaps were filled with shadow. This black network or map resisted the light. I had no need to strain my imagination. I knew the water had fallen on her from above, flowing over her shoulders and breasts, that individual drops had splashed onto the walls, that some of them had been absorbed forever into the porous structure of the material; I knew that before the water finally disappeared down the disgusting rectangular hole of the drain it must have touched the wood, soaked into it, and left some elementary particles there. After all, her body was like memory, collecting invisible yet real particles from the world, absorbing them during the sweltering days and sultry nights, saving them with her sweat, gathering them somewhere deep inside and assimilating them till they became her herself: dust, looks, someone else's touch, pollen, the smell of bedsheets, the stuffy air of the village, other people, light, even the landscape, images of objects she used and those she walked past—all this entered into her, passing through her springy, acquisitive skin, then later, transformed and no longer needed, it would reappear on the surface in the form of dirt and tiredness, and flow away as it did that day in the golden glare of the afternoon, dispersing and returning to the world, which happened to have taken on the form of a shower cubicle, because after all the world has to take on shapes that are accessible to the mind and the senses, otherwise we'd die of longing without ever actually comprehending why we're dying.

So there I stood, almost motionless, performing my blasphemous parody of her being. The faucets were made of black ebonite and had no distinguishing features. A broken match lay on the plastic soap shelf. Its brown head had faded and stained the wooden stem pink. I stood almost stock-still. I was afraid I'd disturb the air, and the air would disturb the rest. Because it was all like a living grave, like something put to sleep forever.

At that moment the bell in the little wooden church started ringing. It was the six o'clock Mass, said for a few old women in dark head scarves for whom only two candles were lit on the altar, the sacristan doing the job of the altar boys. I stepped out very slowly, backward, closing the curtain behind me. I retreated till I felt the wall.

Outside, a woman in a drab-colored apron stood with a mop and bucket, talking to a fat man. I passed between them, interrupting their conversation. When I was a few yards further on I heard the cleaning lady's raised voice: "What did I tell you, boss? The little buggers come in here to take a piss, they do . . ."

The man made some reply, but the woman wasn't convinced and kept repeating what she'd said, though I couldn't hear the words anymore. I walked slowly. Under the metal overhang outside the café there were only locals. The next day I was leaving. Today I was supposed to pack.

That other day, before D. and I headed for Komańcza, we took a turn around the market square in Dukla. There wasn't a living soul. Everyone had either joined the funeral procession or they were at home waiting for the others to come back, so there'd be someone to talk to. D. peered through a dark window into a bicycle repair shop. He called me over. "There's some kind of trumpet in there," he said. "With the bicycles?" I asked, and looked in. It was true—on the wall of the workshop, among the frames, pedals and everything else there was something golden, though you couldn't tell if it was a trombone or a French horn. In any case it shone there, golden and mysterious, and somehow sad and lonely, since all the other brass instruments were at the funeral. It was as if it had stayed behind as a punishment, or because of old age.

After that I wanted to show D. the big veranda and the mansion and we crossed in front of the buildings to find the little passage that led down a few steps to the Dukielka. As we were passing a low wall on the corner of the square, a figure sprang out at us like a jack-in-the-box from behind the wall, landed plumb on its two feet right in front of us, and asked for a cigarette. We didn't even have time to notice if it was a guy or a girl, it was all hairy and curly and indistinct from alcohol. Whoever it was took four smokes "for my girlfriend" and disappeared just as energetically back behind the wall. It was only the shaking of the bushes on the other side that made us believe the incident had been real.

Then later I was drawn to those steps, which seemed to lead underground. It was what was left of a public lavatory. The old wooden door hung off its hinges. I went inside. There was nothing there, just semidarkness and ruins. Nothing whole, just bits and pieces. Places where faucets had been, rusty marks left from fittings, porcelain shards of toilets, and everywhere flakes of paint from the walls. Dust, cobwebs, scraps of newspaper, broken glass, disintegrating red oddments of iron, rubble, and dried shit. And gray light from a small street-level window. Outside the day was sunny, but in here the brightness failed. There are places like that, but they usually appear in dreams. I suddenly felt a twinge of fright. Or rather horror, the cold touch of the oldest fear. It must have been more or less what people felt when they became aware of the existence of time, when they realized they were immobile, that they were being left behind and nothing could ever be done about it.

I stood without moving; my skin crept. In this abandoned, decay-filled john I'd seen matter in its ultimate state of collapse and abandonment. The minutes and years had simply entered into things and broken them from within. The same thing that always happens everywhere. I'd had to live for thirty-six years to have come this far.

With heart in mouth, my spine tingling, I headed up again. I climbed slowly, one step after another, back to the street. The bells of Mary Magdalene were ringing. It was then that I decided to describe it all.

II.

I always wanted to write a book about light. I never could find anything else more reminiscent of eternity. I never was able to imagine things that don't exist. That always seemed a waste of time to me, just like the stubborn search for the Unknown, which only ever ends up looking like an assemblage of old, familiar things in slightly souped-up form. Events and objects either come to an end, or perish, or collapse under their own weight, and if I observe them and describe them it's only because they refract the brightness, shape it, and give it a form that we're capable of comprehending.

The train station at Jasło was well lit and deserted. The sun was shining for the first time in a week. The trains looked benign. It's almost always like that at provincial stations: the cars remind you of the toy train set from your childhood, and the locomotives display their vivid original colors in the glare—green, black, the red of the wheel spokes and the plaque bearing eagle and engine number.

When it's hot, the brown ties give off a nostalgic smell that makes you long to take a journey without a destination, moving slowly and tediously across a still, ornamental landscape. You can get out, cross the tracks where it's not permitted, in full view of the conductor in his raspberry-red cap, and nothing happens. The cars have white signboards on their sides with place-names: Zagórz, Zagórzany, Krynica, or Khyriv over the Ukrainian border, where fat women are waiting to take the same train when it comes back; they'll be lugging stacks of knockoff Cubans, spirits, and packs of pirate Pall Malls, so as to sell it all in Krościenko and head back home the same day.

The air has a golden tinge. The poplars and birches are in blossom. Dust hovers over the station like a mild narcotic. The ticket costs two zlotys something, while the journey is eighteen miles or so and will take the best part of an hour.

The compartment was empty, as was the whole train, it seemed. It smelled of stale cigarette smoke, while exhaust fumes from the diesel locomotive drifted in through the window. To the north, on the far side of the valley of the Jasiółka, lay the ridges of the Strzyżów heights. The leafless beech woods shone in the sun like ruddy fur. I was going to Dukla yet again. There were people working in the fields. The plowed earth looked like chocolate. They were sowing, harrowing, planting, lone women leaning on their hoes and following the train with their eyes. Some of them were simply sitting facing the sun, half-leaning in repose, their legs spread, propped on an elbow, stretched out like heterothermic animals in the too-early heat. Insectlike vehicles constructed from old WSK motorbikes—three wheels, engine whining at its highest possible rpm, and a flat trailer drawn behind at walking pace—were ascending the hillside. Loaded with grain or bricks of saltpeter, they crawled over the muddy ground beneath the blue sky like docile beasts of a newly domesticated species. There were a mechanical specialty of the poorer regions. Some had a regular little cart instead of a trailer. They were a transitional hybrid, halfway between horse-drawn plow and tractor. They paused at the highest point, the men strapped on a canvas apron, then they walked downhill sowing by hand like in the old days, in a dancelike rhythm: step, broad fling, step, take a handful, step, broad fling. I was in the train smoking, yet despite the distance I could hear the noise of their rubber boots as they trod heavily, a resonant sound that was a little like a slap, a little like flesh.

So it was. Barely half a mile a minute, so everything lasted long enough in the air that it could take hold in the memory, leaving an impression like the millions of other images that you then carry inside yourself, and that's why people are like crazy stereoscopes, and life is like a hallucination, because nothing that you see is what it is. Something's always showing through from underneath, rising to the surface like a drop of olive oil, opalescent, glistening, luring you like a fiendish trick, a will-o'-the-wisp, a temptation without end. It's impossible to touch anything without disturbing something else. Like in an old house where a single quiet step sets glass rattling in a cabinet two rooms away. That's how the mind works, how it protects you from madness, because life would be impossible if events were lodged in time like a nail hammered into the wall. The spiderweb of memory enwraps the head, thanks to which the present is equally hazy, and you can be confident it'll turn almost entirely painlessly into the past.

In Tarnowiec white clouds hung over the station. From the horizontal gaps between them a golden mist descended onto a wall bearing the inscription "Sendecja are Jewz." The old-fashioned railway signals were lowered. I wanted to select an event from my life, but for the moment none seemed better than any other.

Then four men got into the compartment next to mine. I'd seen them walking along the deserted platform. They looked like workers who'd managed to get off before the factory whistle blew. They were like children playing hooky. Through the thin partition I could hear them moving about, vigorously and casually making themselves comfortable, perhaps putting their feet up on the seats, and I immediately smelled cheap Klubowe cigarettes. Before the train even pulled out they were deep in a lively conversation. They were talking about televisions, the way boys talk about cars, about mythical makes, imaginary specifications, miraculous capabilities. Sony, Samsung, Curtis, Panasonic, Phillips . . . But it didn't sound like the usual unthinking latter-day incantations. The guys were speaking about the different kinds of light emitted from various sorts of screens. This one was too cold, that one too purple, a third one too brilliant and unreal, painful to the human eye; another kind was too soft, sugary-sweet, an insult to the natural dignity of the colors of light. They were seeking an ideal, combining the qualities of different electronic mechanisms the way you mix paints, or spend hours setting up the lights on a film set so as for one brief moment to capture reality in a single unique and unrepeatable second, when for the blink of an eye it coincides with the imagination. They were trying to reach a compromise between the visible and the represented. There wasn't a word about things technical, not an ounce of doltish idolatry. At least till Jedlicze, where they got out amid the silvery purification columns wrapped in labyrinths of refinery piping. Maybe the conversation continued? Maybe they were on their way to work in that technoscape, at the edge of which, without a care in the world, cows were grazing, horses working, and age-old poverty was slowly turning into a rustic *paysage*.

And so it was all the way to Krosno.

In the distance, with titillating inscriptions on their red and yellow tarpaulins, huge trucks move along: the glistening projectiles of Volvo tankers, green Mercedes vans, DAF articulated truck-trailers, polished Jelczes, snow-white Scanias, and among them the small fry of regular automobiles like lesser stones in the necklace of capitalism: amethysts, emeralds, rubies, opals, sapphires—all in sunlight, glinting, from east to west and back again, all the way across Europe with a sticky squeal of rubber on heated asphalt, with fat guys at the wheel in leather jackets, a

Marlboro between their lips and the Blaupunkt cranked up to the max, pedal to the metal like they were being chased by the devil, or they were chasing him (who knows), as though amid the ancient unmoving hills time had hollowed out a narrow passageway in which it could accelerate as if it intended to make up for entire centuries, leave everything behind and get to somewhere outside of material, inhabited space. That was how it looked.

On the hillsides, on flat patches along the road, at the edges of alder thickets, the locals stood and watched as their world broke off like a piece of land or an ice floe and drifted backward, though it looked as if it was staying in place. The iron harrows on the wagons, the pitchforks, harnesses, rubber boots on bare feet, the symbiotic smells of stable and home, the powerful age-old interweaving of human and animal existence, curdled milk, potatoes, eggs, lard, no long journeys in search of trophies, no miracles or legends other than satiety and a peaceful death. They stood there, leaning on the wooden helves of their implements, rooted in the earth that would soon shake them off the way a dog shakes off water. The trembling brightly colored line of the highway ran along the bottom of the valley. In essence it was a tectonic crack, a geological fault between epochs. They were standing there watching. At least, they ought to have been. In reality they were just getting on with their work without a trace of interest, without fear, entirely engrossed in the materiality of the world, its weight, which enabled them to feel their own existence as something real.

That was how it was as I rode the train to Dukla in April, the light continually summoning things into being then annihilating them again with a cold, supernatural indifference. The outskirts of Krosno were flat and industrial. Warehouses, sheds, lockups, general devastation. There was something lying by the tracks. Maybe someone had been supposed to load it up and take it away, but now it didn't look like it would be worth the effort. Branch lines ran off amid low buildings. They were coated in rust. Scrub, nooks and corners, the smell of hot tar roofs—just the place to sit yourself down, drink cheap fruit wine, and watch the long-distance trains that no one ever gets on. Sun-drenched walls, benches made of a handful of bricks and a plank, the glitter of green and brown broken glass, white bottle caps, colorful tongues of trash slithering down the embankments, and a girl of twelve in her mother's high heels pushing an enameled stroller that was fifteen years old. Railroad suburbs always look like a no-man's-land—no one either lives or works here, so everything's permissible, while the lazy trains, either gathering speed or slowing down, give off an unreal aura, and everything is plunged in the half-sleep of the borderland between childhood and adulthood, where dreams and reality cannot be told apart.

The Magnum Disco Night Club Roundhouse was empty inside. The openwork glass rotunda had shared the fate of the rest of the neighborhood. The only thing left from when the place had been open was the sign. Though in fact you couldn't tell if there'd ever been any action here. Maybe it was still to come? It looked as much like a renovation as a demolition. A glass-built soap bubble growing out of a patch of ground strewn with scrap iron and concrete—the slightest prick and there'd be nothing left but empty space. I tried to imagine a night out under that pathetic dome, in the morbid quiver of strobe lighting, with a rumble of trains behind your back. The image I got was of a terrarium, or a dance of skeletons.

The conductor came by, but he didn't ask for my ticket. He just said, "We'll be there soon." As if I looked like a newcomer, like someone who needed help.

I had an hour till the bus for Dukla. Too long to wait, too short for a decent walk, just enough time for a veal cutlet in the Smerf Café, where up till then I'd never seen another soul, though it was very reasonably priced, clean, you could get a meal no less tasty than the national average for around thirty thousand zlotys. The time was also just right for a beer at the store with the one outside table, the place to the right beyond the post office, along with a guy who'd wheeled his bike into the beer garden and leaned it against the table, though it was an old Ural with a leather saddle like on a Cossack horse, and a spring shaped like an electric heating coil.

Then later, on the bus, I thought about how Dukla deserved a rail connection. If not a proper one, than at least a narrow-gauge line. Once or twice a day a little locomotive would roll up to a low gravel-covered platform somewhere between Węgierski Trakt and the bus station. The tracks would divide the old part of town from the flashy nouveau-riche neighborhood copied from TV shows and things remembered from seasonal labor in the Reich. Not tracks even, just one track and a passing place, say, in Miejsce Piastowe. The hard, insistent clatter, wooden seats in narrow cars with windows that instead of handles have leather grips like on a suitcase. Smoking's allowed on the entire train, it makes no difference at all, because the south wind from over the pass blows coal smoke in through every crack and crevice. From Krosno it takes a good two hours, bouncing up and down, with the rattle of couplings and the sideways swaying, so every once in a while you have to go out on the observation platform to rest your bones, and there in unmown ditches skinny cows are being grazed by children, because it's high summer, school vacation, and a landscape without a cowherd is a fearful wrong.

A completely separate line, then. Tickets can only be purchased from a conductor in a uniform with facings bearing Dukla's coat of arms—three black-and-gold horns on a white background. The cars would absolutely have to be dark green, faded, and old. The locomotive could only be black, a little rusty, well oiled, with red spokes swollen from the effort, and decorated with the Dukla coat of arms on the front of the boiler. Everything as it once used to be, like in a transparent dream where ribbons of time and memory are superimposed on one another like a consolation for a too-short life. Cigarettes with a mouthpiece instead of a filter, in hard cardboard boxes with a sphinx on the lid, or with no mouthpiece, but pressed flat, like the Hungarian Munkás brand. Pants had to be pressed and appropriately wide, while in the pocket of your jacket there should be a flat bottle with an inscription on its bottom reading: Baczewski Distillery of Vodkas and Spirits, Lwów. And a Panama hat. What else? Probably the line should end in Dukla. Right next to the place where there's a bakery kiosk now; the rails come to a stop at a huge wooden buffer on iron girders. Beyond that there's nothing.

It's funny that, in wrestling with time, we usually end up returning to what's past, to what already has shape, to a ready-made form. The imagination is incapable of inventing anything. When it's suspended in a vacuum it plummets like a stone, or entertains itself, which in the end amounts to the same thing.

I dreamed my sentimental, narrow-gauge, fin-de-siècle dream in the crowded bus to Jasionka. People gave off their smells. Two girls behind were talking about zits. "See, I just got it this morning." "Then squeeze it." "I'm not sure." To the right, the historic derricks of Bóbrka stood on the hills. Then, somewhere near Równe, Cergowa Mountain came into view. From the north it looks like an animal: huge layered head and back arching as if it were about to rise to its feet. There's no trace of gentle Soracte. You can't help expecting a heavy grunt or a gasp. A legendary beast—indolent, temperamental, with a coarse coat of pine forest. "I mean, you can't walk around with it all white like that." A moment later there was a stop and they left by the rear door, so I didn't get a look.

The first thing I noticed was that the "one-fifty" was gone from in front of the Cistercian monastery. The immense forty-ton mobile gun had vanished along with its plinth. It had stood there for thirty years, and now it had disappeared without a trace. Where it had been, outside the monastery, bulldozers and backhoes were bustling to and fro. They'd taken a bite out of the cemetery hill. The bus drove on, but I promised myself I'd locate my cannon.

Later on I found out it had been removed after a town referendum. Seventy-seven votes for removal, eleven against. A sorry end.

There was scaffolding on the face of the building with the jeweler's store. The place was being renovated. The sidewalks had been leveled out. Some were entirely new. Children were painting the school fence green. I felt like the ground was beginning to slip from under my feet. Opposite the ruined synagogue goats were grazing as before, but there too something was going on. Behind the chain-link fence that surrounded the temple there lay newly milled timber, planks, beams, as if someone was planning to build something. I walked around the perimeter of the market square, because it wasn't like it usually was. It was completely different, though I couldn't put my finger on exactly why. A poster announced that on Sunday there was going to be a game, tickets were two zlotys, reduced cost one zloty, "women and children free." Alongside was a notice saying that in the cinema, at 10:00 A.M., there was going to be a recitation contest devoted to Blessed John of Dukla. In my guidebook I read that John "brought many dissenters into the bosom of the Catholic Church. In this way he was before his time, sensing as he did the need for ecumenicalism."

It was hot. I was looking for somewhere to cool down. I went to Mary Magdalene. Inside, children were having a rehearsal for their first communion. The parents were sitting in back, watching their boys and girls walk up to the priest one by one and light imaginary candles from the priest's pretend flame. The cleric reminded them that on the actual day the flame would be real. I left the church. Outside the doorway a woman in a lilac-pink dress took a lilac-pink pack of Weston lights from a lilac-pink bag. I was restless. I'd clearly come at the wrong time. I hadn't even glanced at Amalia.

In front of the Cistercian monastery two men in dog collars were arranging a visiting group of boys for a photograph. I passed to the side so as not to get in their way. Inside, there were two movie cameras going, and a monk in a brown habit was explaining something. One camera was pointing at him, the other roamed the ceiling, which showed scenes from the life of Blessed John. I went out into the courtyard. The sun-heated white flagstones smelled of wax and gasoline. The bulldozers and backhoes had fallen still. The workers were eating lunch and drinking from plastic bottles. Outside the post office there were new telephone booths that were bluer than the sky. The boys were getting into a bus with Rzeszów plates. I went slowly downhill. The only thing left was the bar at the tourist office.

It was empty, empty as never before, and in some unprecedented way, because everything seemed to be in its place, as if waiting, yet the utter absence of anything whatsoever turned that expectation into something ideal, empty, and cold as a hieroglyph. I had the impression that even the dust had stopped settling, and the murmurs of the bar solidified in the air and lingered. I sat in the place where Andrzej Niewiadomski often sat. The lady brought my beer out to me, as though the bar had table service now. As usual in Dukla, I had a Leżajsk. The beer went down without resistance, but that was all that could be said for it. It hid itself in exactly the place where it ought to come out into the open. It was just a chill in the belly and an increasing heaviness, as if I were going to remain in that wooden hall forever, remain in Dukla, become part of it, its property, like the everyday shadows of objects, of the trees on the square, the houses, and the people hurrying to catch the morning bus to Krosno.

And in the very middle of the bright day I suddenly felt the heresy of existence, a bizarre unsticking, the blister between the skin of the world and the self, which absorbs consciousness like the plasma left after a burn, and so the wound never fully dries, except perhaps while we're asleep, but at those times we have no awareness of it. Sluggish and motionless, my thoughts fading, I was heading for materiality. I imagined myself cooling and irreversibly hardening, and the light beginning to take me over, like all other things that have assumed their permanent form. Entirely immersed in the grace of sunlight, free, devoid of any capabilities whatsoever, I remain at the table, my hand on the empty glass; I'm as empty as it is, and in two hundred years someone will find me here, to their chagrin, because they'll have to weave a web of conjectures, patch together a story to fill out their own mind, to rid themselves of the inner echo, make use of what's been given them, what they're fated to have, while I am far beyond all that, beyond the need for any kind of alternative, I'm merely a thing that people have to deal with, just as now I myself have to quarrel with every moment, with the image and shimmer of the world at 3:15 P.M. in April, making use of any available means, because in reality not one of them actually exists.

And then an old man in a stained gray jacket came in and sat at the next table. He did nothing else, didn't order anything, and for sure he couldn't have been meeting anyone there. He lit a cigarette and stared out the window through the smoke. He was one of those people who resemble mineral matter. Movement is not their natural state. They go from stillness to stillness. Just as though they've already accomplished everything and now they're spending time in the purest sense of that phrase. They're letting it pass them by, maybe even flow through them.

So the old man sat there and the barmaid didn't mind. At rare intervals he moved his lips to take a loud puff at his cigarette, which he held close up to his mouth. He didn't look lost in thought. Stray images were likely coming to him from the past, flooding his mind and rescuing it from the present. At moments of perfect rest we never see the future—imagining it requires an effort of will. Only the past comes unbeckoned, because old, transparent events are no longer capable of hurting the body. They protect it from an abrupt fall into the future.

The sun moved across the sky outside the window. Its gentle golden touch reached the dull fabric of the man's jacket, and soon his whole figure was suspended in space as if on the verge of vanishing. The past of recollections and the eternal present of light took him into their possession and gently annihilated him.

So then, the magnifying glass of Dukla, an opening in the earth, in the body, in time. The dark space between the eyepiece and the lens of the telescope. The gloom in which events and objects solidify, then cast their reflection on the polished surfaces of beginning and end.

I pulled myself together and left the bar. The heat-swollen afternoon was splitting in places, and early evening shadows were beginning to appear in the cracks. People were coming out of apartment buildings just like that, with no obligations, simply to chat, have a smoke, and take a look at how their town had changed since the morning or the day before. After-dinner fullness, open windows with music playing on the radio, and the calm stooping figures of winos huddled on street corners in whispered consultations concerning Bieszczadzkie wine with the sideways picture of the black bear on its label. I was drawn to Amalia.

This time I was lucky. There was no one else there. The empty church still smelled of children, but the air had already returned to its place in the recesses of the ceiling, and it abided there like still waters. The wooden pews were the color of ivory.

She was lying there as always. Delicate, small, submerged in frills, sleeping. She could actually have been taken for a little girl, if it weren't for the slender, adult shape of her shoe. Two large mirrors on the walls of the chapel reflected her as though someone had once taken fright at such a tangible female presence and decided to render her a little less real, more sleepy. For a place of worship, this proliferation of images was decidedly too worldly. It hinted at an error, an illusion, or simply a mild form of madness. I thought to myself that with its patroness, its reflections, its fictions, and its Amalia, this church was more human than it might appear.

Yes indeed. I touched anything that aroused my curiosity. I was alone. The light from the high window, the reflected glimmer in the mirrors, and the fragrant penumbra of the nave deprived my movements of any realness. The black marble of the sarcophagus was warm and smooth.

And then I recalled all the churches I'd ever been in. Clearest of all I saw the ones furthest back, the first ones, those where mystery had been given visible form. Our Lady in blue, with a pink indifferent face, in the church on Szembek in Warsaw: this was the first image of a woman that I remembered *as* an image. It was also my first image of a supernatural being. In my six-year-old mind those two things became combined in the strangest way, creating a heady mixture that used to numb me during the tedious sixty minutes of Mass. The half-naked alabaster figure of Christ hung there in absolute calm. The few delicate wounds on his sculpted waxen body confirmed my conviction that His death was a gentle, almost elegant act.

Streetcars drove up and down Grochowska. Balconies rusted above street level. The bodywork of cars was matted. This world and that were made of similar matter. They differed only in execution. A manifold, proletarian version of the Holy Spirit as a dove rose into the air over the shacks of Kawcza, Osiecka, and Zamieniecka Streets. Guys with rags on the end of sticks stood on the roofs of the dovecotes, driving their flocks from one end of the sky to the other. At that time everything took flesh once and for all, and no thought today could separate those things, not even the cleverest sophistry could alter it, this blood of blood and bone of bone, because reality had swallowed a symbol, and the symbol had grown the plumage of reality. And standing there at Amalia's tomb, in a split second I understood that back then, in that first of all times, all invisible things had been crammed into wooden or stone forms along with space and color, and everything that followed was merely fiction threaded over the core of the real the way cotton candy is wound around a wooden stick, and when all is said and done it's only the stick that's left, and in your belly there's only a sweet emptiness. And when all's said and done everything comes down to the most intimate forms, to your own body and its variations in the bodies of others, and no other form of expression can be found, because it would be unbelievable or incomprehensible.

The church on Szembek, then, was made of the same thing as everything else. When you walked out of it you entered a space that was somewhat more rarefied, but identical. This blasphemous unity was the condition for everyday wonder. On top of everything, the sensuality of this religion made it accessible to animals and plants, with that strange rhythm of warm and cold stretches in the nave of the temple, with the slow and ceremonious alternation of light and dark as Sunday passed over Grochów. Signs descended from heaven and sought entry into the human body. So it was.

We'd go home on foot. We'd drop by the cake shop, where the walls bore pictures of muscular brown men. Black slaves on a cocoa plantation, perhaps, or maybe sand diggers by the Vistula. This question has been bothering me for thirty years. Whenever I eat a doughnut, I see a sulfur-yellow wall and those chocolate-colored figures. I'll never know who they really were.

Then we'd enter the yard outside our building. I'd change out of my Sunday best and I was free till lunchtime. The dumpster, nooks and crannies, soot-blackened lids of the coal chutes, rubble, odds and ends of junk, weeds, the swelter of a city summer under a light blue covering of sky. The same sun shone on Szembek, on the church, and on the wooden john in the corner of the yard. It passed through the stained glass windows, and through our skin. The same sun brings to life Amalia's body in my mind, the same glare smears events on the slide of memory, mixes them like drops of colored liquid from childhood games: green was made with grass, blue out of paint scratched from the wall, yellow from sand.

So I was alone. The heated silvery sheen of the mirrors mingled with the dense afternoon light. Warm shadows were gathering in the folds of her gown. Steps rang out near the entrance and immediately fell silent. Someone had knelt down or sat in a pew. The taut soft space conveyed sounds unaltered. They were like objects. The foot in its gray shoe was so small I could almost have enclosed it in my hand. I thought to myself that in a few days, in May, when the leaves on the trees outside the chapel will have opened, every gust of wind would change this interior: glassy little shoots of chiaroscuro, trembling veinlets of sunlight, stretching into the warm mottled air—all this would multiply the unreal aura of brilliance and death to the very limits of illusion, where the truest desires are born. That's right, one more week, I thought. In May it would all be different. Even more deceptive and alluring. Just like those days thirty years ago when my mother and I would climb a metal ladder into a tarpaulin-covered truck somewhere on Wileńska. It was called a work car. At daybreak, Lublins and Stars would gather men from Radzymin and Piława and Wyszków and take them to work at the FSO automobile plant, then in the afternoon they'd be driven back to their villages. You sat on wooden benches without a backrest. The truck bounced and jolted, it smelled of gasoline and sweat and cigarettes. In an hour we were there.

For the longest time I thought I was walking by a real river. I'd stand on the bank and stare over to the other side, which was overgrown with willows. My bank was the edge of a huge sandy flatland. The closer it got to the water, the more desertlike it became. Far off in the distance all the cows from the village were grazing, there must have been a meadow there, but by the water there were only sharp knifelike grasses that cut till you bled. The village lay beyond the dune hills. Some of the houses were perched on the hillside. They were wood-built, brown, some were thatched. On hot days the water gave off a marshy, fishy smell mingled with the acrid tannin aroma of the willows. A row of giant poplars at the edge of the village regularly attracted lightning. The hot, loose sand turned every walk into a laborious trek. From the farms came the scent of pine and aspen smoke. It joined with the damp air from the river and lingered permanently in long horizontal skeins, even at night, after all the stoves had been put out. You had to climb a hill, pass by fences of black paling that guarded the heroic vegetable gardens, and you'd come out onto the main road of the village, with its hot draft of air that drew in the smells of all the farmyards, of decay and animals and living things, stirred them together, macerated them, and even at noon, when emptiness and stillness prevailed on the highway, it was impossible to avoid the presence of all the people, the livestock, the objects, that occupied the houses and yards. It spread, pushing between sky and earth and the irregular buildings like a ponderous, replete, invisible serpent.

My grandfather was a firefighter. He had an antique gold helmet with a crest. He also served as chairman of the village council. There was a red sign that hung on the house. As a reward for exemplary discharge of his duties he was given a big fat book entitled *The Paris Commune*. It contained a multitude of illustrations. They were stippled with mold. The same went for the raspberry-red cloth binding. The book lay in the woodshed. I never saw my grandfather reading it. I was the only one that looked at it. It's quite possible it was never honored with a place on the shelf where other books were kept. There were very few of them, and I don't remember any of the titles. I remember pretty much everything, or at least I'm able to imagine everything. But not those books, though they were definitely there. They evidently lacked a sufficiently distinct smell.

My grandfather was extremely religious. Something along the lines of Mary Month devotions took place at his house in May. In the main room a little altar was set up on the dresser: geraniums in pots wrapped in white crepe, paper flowers, thick metal candlesticks with yellow candles, and a dim, smoke-darkened copy of the Black Madonna of Częstochowa. The womenfolk would gather. I never saw any men. They'd come in headscarves, wearing worn-down men's slippers on their bare feet, or black sandals with straps. It wasn't a big village, and so somehow or other there was room for them all in the living room. Plus, of course, not all of them came, certainly not the younger ones. Grandfather would light the candles, cross himself, say a prayer, then begin the litany. He was a stern, hard-working man. He was constantly in motion, always in dark blue drill overalls, forever engrossed in tasks that never had any beginning or end, because he probably didn't remember ever being in a state of inaction. He was slim, with a lean, oval face. I liked him and I was afraid of his temper. I got the idea that brusqueness was a quality all old men had in common. Like the rugged, patriarchal tenderness he'd sometimes allow himself of an evening when there were no more jobs to do. He'd take me on his lap and laugh. He may well have been amused by the fact that something so small, frail, and useless could even exist.

His denim overshirt was so thoroughly impregnated with all the smells of the world that he himself had become hard to separate out from it and I was unable to imagine him traveling away, crossing the gray-green frontier of the landscape. When he sat in the summer kitchen in the evening, his figure was saturated with the entire day that had just passed. He was followed inside by the dry dusty air of the barn, hot horse sweat, the stuffy ammoniacal odor of the cattle shed, the cold chill of the cellar, and the resinous mist of the pine grove if that day he'd happened to have been gathering firewood. All this mingled with the scent of places and objects my own skin had come into contact with: the dark walkway between the house and the fence, where the dense foliage let no light through even at noon, though if you pushed aside the vertical branches of lilac you had a blinding view of the neighbor's yard, where unsuspecting people were bustling around. I knew them, but they still looked garish and strange, as if I were peering at the next world. The earth was sandy and chill. Then you turned right, the shade came to an end, the sun-warmed vegetable garden gave off edible aromas mixed with the metallic smell of the weeds that twined around the fence and were left to grow, so they rose higher and higher, encircling the garden in a ring of coolness. The gate was rickety. The glassed-in veranda concentrated the heat like a magnifying glass, but three steps away you could find the permanent cool of a wooden house in which the stove hadn't been lit since spring. Geranium pots stood in the small windows, so there was a smell of semidarkness and decay, and the light was so rarefied that every object seemed to live only thanks to its own feeble glow. The mirror on the wall hung at an angle and never reflected what you thought it would. Likewise the wedding picture: it leaned over my six-year-old self, looking not straight ahead but slightly down from above. On the black bed there was a pile of bedding with a Gypsy woman in a sequined dress on top; one time I looked under the dress, but found only an overcast stitch along the seam of a little sack filled with sawdust. The floor creaked wetly and softly. The insides of the drawers in the shadowy dresser were unexpectedly light, planed, smelling of mothballs and whiteness, with a faint whiff of river mud, because the wind couldn't entirely blow it out of the sheets. The air was still. The walls green. Even when people came in, nothing changed in that atmosphere formed once and forever.

It was in that very room my grandfather conducted his miniature services in May. He would be wearing a white shirt. He'd kneel at the decorated dresser, and that position, so unnatural for his figure of constant motion, made me uneasy. His bronzed hands would poke from tightly fastened cuffs and do nothing. I listened to his rough voice, which on normal days issued instructions, grumbled, cursed. "O tower of ivory," "Thou golden home," "Thou Ark of the Covenant," "O city of wisdom," "Thou pure virgin." He pronounced all these extraordinary, extravagant, exotic words in the same way he named things in the everyday world.

Sternly, without inflection, as if indicating old, familiar objects. There were tears in his eyes. The women would respond with their loose, many-voiced "Pray for us," moving toward the final syllable, which marked the rhythm. I would be kneeling by the wall, reflecting on the meaning of the images of tower, ark, city, and virgin. I was unable to resolve the contradictions. On my grandfather's lips the words sounded frivolous, almost indecent. The splitting of his concrete existence and the fiction to which he lent his thoroughly material voice made me blush. I was simply embarrassed, because I'd taken him for a sober and serious man, while here he was, addressing something that was utterly nonexistent, and in addition was very clearly a woman. I felt I had been betrayed by reality.

I would wait till it was all over, then run down to the river. On the horizon, a thin green line attached the earth to the sky. The sand was still warm, and there wasn't a soul to be seen. The blue air of evening was rising over the plain. Here under the immense sky things retained their places and their meaning. Two flat-bottomed boats lay motionless on the water. A cow was lowing somewhere. I peed in the sand and watched it darken. I was small, my little shorts didn't even have a zipper. I walked directly east with my shadow stretched out in front of me. I wandered a long way, then suddenly got scared and came back.

The sun had gone. It had disappeared behind the back of the village, which now stood there, black and two-dimensional, like a stage set. Somewhere in the distance a motionless fire was burning, illuminating nothing. I felt a dark fear, because I couldn't make out any point of entry, no crack or crevice by which I might return. It was as if the entire landscape aside from me had turned into antimatter, and my grandfather, the house, the farmyard, and everything else had been imprisoned in it, or even worse, had actually become it. I knew I'd lost it all and I was unable to move. It was only when night moved away from the houses and washed over me like dark water that I started to run in that direction.

Right now I'm trying to arrange the whole thing into some kind of sequence, though I remember only fragments, the imprint of objects on the space of those times, though of course not the objects themselves, with their unrepeatable texture of scratches, cracks, wrinkles. What comes to me now are only their traces, phantoms of originals that stop halfway between existence and naming. They're like touched-up funeral photographs.

In any case, I more or less made it through those last long vacations. The goose shit mixed in with the sand looked like greenish Plasticine. There was a smell of nettles in the narrow walkway behind the stables. The sun-warmed wall made the aroma intensify during the day, till by two or three in the afternoon it had the concentrated force of a hallucination. It was hard to distinguish the smell from the stinging touch of the leaves. I'd go there to watch two teenage girls. They lived on the other side of the fence. The younger one was white, fleshy, not yet fully formed. A little like she'd been born too soon and the air had fixed her unfinished features for good. She was entirely normal, just a little unshaped.

The other girl had a dark, slim body. She was like a boy, or a crude drawing. Her silhouette against the bright expanse of the farmyard looked like a sketchy, mobile symbol. She wore a skimpy red outfit consisting of shorts and a halter top with thin shoulder straps. She would feed the chickens, carry firewood and water, quarrel with her mother. It wasn't much. I'd observe her nimble body without really knowing why. No one ever caught me at it and explained the reasons. In some indistinct yet powerful way I associated it in my unformed and acquisitive mind with the rest of the world: my grandfather would be saying his litany. Scraped-off fish scales would be drying in the grass outside the door of the summer kitchen. The triangular net strung out to dry in the sun was hard and rough. The hazelwood fishing poles were propped in the corner of the veranda, their green lines wrapped around them. When you scratched the dark lead of the sinkers they'd show through silver. The hooks were golden, like the "house" in the prayer. I couldn't come up with any other rendering. "Ivory tower" forever remained something smooth, slender, beguiling. The mind sought refuge from atrophy by taking on a form that accorded with what it was taught about body and soul, while the vacuum of metaphors immediately sucked in various elements, kneading them and fashioning them in its own likeness. In this way the tanned girl next door incarnated the "pure and most wonderful virgin" so exactly that I found her features in the pictures that fell from black prayer books, of which there were five or six in my grandfather's house. The red edges of the cards had the same color as her skimpy clothes.

I was startled by the same young priest as before. I hadn't heard him come up. He stopped at the entrance to the side chapel. I think he was surprised to find me there. I looked neither like a tourist nor a parishioner. My hand was still touching Amalia's shoe. He cleared his throat and raised his hand to his mouth. He was as embarrassed as I was. He waited for me to leave the chapel, then half closed the grate that separated it from the nave. Perhaps he used to go there to look at Amalia too. If I were him I certainly would have. I could feel his eyes watching me leave; I breathed a sigh of relief when I emerged onto the street. I crossed the roadway and to cover my tracks I bought a pack of Moldovan cigarettes from a Ukrainian peddler woman for one zloty. The red-and-cream box from Chişinău bore a warning in two languages: *Fumatul dauneazasanatatis dumneavoastra*, and *kurenie opasno dlya vashogo zdarovia*. The woman had traveled three hundred miles to be able to sit on the Dukla sidewalk. The world is filled with details that provide the beginnings of stories.

I strolled over to the market square, sat on a bench, and took out one of the cigarettes. It was characterless and crumbly. Its taste reminded me of all those old cigarettes that grown men used to smoke. Wawels, Dukats, Giewonts with their low-grade paper, in packs that were like clumsy dreams about the faraway world. We used to steal them, or pick up unfinished butts. Around the edges they'd be sort of brown, and dark from saliva. Grown-upness had a very literal taste. Our spit mingled with the spit of men. It may well have acted like a vaccine, a kind of existential homeopathy, protecting us from a too abrupt fall into adulthood.

But this was supposed to be about Dukla . . .

For several years now I've been trying to figure out the nature of its strange pull. My thoughts sooner or later always end up right here, as if in this handful of little streets they were going to find satisfaction, whereas in fact they're suspended in a vacuum. Cergowska, Zielona, Nadbrzeżna, Parkowa, Podwale, the market square. Three bars, two churches, two bridges, a bus station, a handful of stores, and the Museum of Brotherhood in Arms. A photography studio and two veterinary doctors. Just enough so human space retains its continuity, just enough for the traveler to feel he's headed in a familiar direction, while pure geography barely shows through from under topography.

So then, Dukla as a memento, a mental hole in the soul, a key that cannot be copied, a spirit overgrown with the glittering plumage of the real. Dukla worthy of a litany, Dukla with the moldering body of Amalia in place of a heart, Dukla filled with space in which images lie down and are overtaken by the past, while the future ceases to be of interest, and I could sit on the west side of the market square to the point of stupefaction, till utter dementia set in, like a village idiot, a bumpkin Buddhist, a jack of clubs tossed from the pack and out of context, like a drunk outside a bar window on which all the wonders of the world are being projected along with the stupidest ideas imaginable, ideas whose very existence no one would even have suspected an hour ago, while behind my back, along the street, in the shade of leafless maple trees, the citizens would be going about their business, trotting between the Kalwaria furniture store, the bookshop, and the market. Actually, that's exactly how it was until I finished the Doina cigarette and decided to go back home via Żmigród, because I wanted to gaze at Cergowa from the rear window of the bus in the honeylike slanting light and do some thinking about Soracte and Lorrain and those tiny human figures under a vast sky, about the desperate defiance with which they clung to the landscape, though the landscape paid no attention to them, even though they were boring into it, digging, altering its shape, skinning it alive, honing the lines of the horizon.

And that was what I did. Ticket inspectors got on in Głojsce. A kid in a fancy jacket put up some resistance, but they dragged him off the bus in Łysa Góra and bundled him into a Polonez that had been following behind. People made a fuss, though they didn't budge from their seats. Loudest of all were the women. "That's no way to treat anyone!" Someone timidly pointed out that the kid hadn't had a ticket. "So what if he didn't! Times are different now! I'm gonna report them. I took down their numbers." But before we reached Żmigród everything was back to normal. Cigarette smoke drifted from the driver's seat, and the distant ridges of Wątkowska Mountain had the same blue tinge as the smoke.

White chickens were poking about on the market square in Żmigród. They wandered among the feet of the people waiting for the Jasło bus. An old man dressed in black with a long gray beard was feeding them breadcrumbs. Before that he'd said hello to everyone. He bowed and shook hands. The children giggled. The old man looked like a real gentleman. Six months earlier I'd seen him in the village of Łosie, thirty miles west of here. At that time he'd been going into a store, greeting people formally in the same way and asking whether anyone had a horse to sell. The guys in berets and rubber boots shifted their weight from one foot to the other and explained apologetically that they weren't farmers, and that generally speaking horses were hard to come by in Łosie. He made quite an impression on people, that elderly gentleman who looked like Walt Whitman and wore a black velvet ribbon in place of a necktie.

This time he sat down on a bench, tipped his hat back on his head, the chickens forming a wreath around him, and an old guy in a cap started up a conversation:

"You come far?"

"From Krempna. Went looking for a horse."

"They didn't have one."

"They did. But it was a gelding. I was after a mare."

"There's not many horses these days. Time'll come there won't be any at all."

"What kind of time will that be, do you think?"

But he never got an answer. He'd also run out of bread, and the chickens wandered away from the bus stop to peck around under the benches on the market square, among some young people who had nothing for them. The boys were giving the girls a drink from their green bottles of Sprite and flicking away their cigarette butts, which the chickens didn't even look at. Leško drove by in his silver Chevrolet, but he didn't notice me there and I didn't manage to wave to him. A broad band of shadow had appeared on the western side of the square. It gave off a chill. The old guy and the elderly gentleman were arguing about whether a world without horses could even exist.

One day it turned out it wasn't a real river. Grandfather and I had rowed to the far side and gone in among the willows. The ground was boggy, warm water standing in stagnant pools. The willows blocked my view, but they only came up to my grandfather's shoulders so he led the way confidently, walking in a straight line. He just glanced back from time to time to make sure I hadn't disappeared in some miry hollow. The tops of his rubber boots knocked against one another with a gentle slap. Dark sweat stains marked his pale blue shirt. My eyes were at the level of his cracked brown belt. Then I caught sight of the glistening mirror of the water, and it was the most boundless thing I'd ever seen in my short life. I was blinded by the immensity of the silvery expanse. I stood at the bank like I was on the edge of a precipice. Birds hovered in the air's vacuum. Seeing them, I felt my head spin. The sky had receded to undetectable heights. I couldn't even see it. This was what a true river looked like. The one I'd been going down to before now was only a narrow arm separated from the main channel by a low willow-covered island. It ran on by itself for a few miles before it rejoined the real stream. It was known as the "Break," you'd say you were going down to the Break. It never shone. It trailed by, greenish and lethargic. The actual river was sprightly, luminous, afire, though in fact its vast size prevented you from seeing whether it was flowing, because the trembling boundary between water and air could only be marked in the imagination. Grandfather pointed and said that that was where he'd been baptized. But I couldn't see anything except vibrant quivering light. The place he was indicating had no beginning and no end. It was filled by an atomized glow. I thought my grandfather must mean the sky, or something like it, and I wasn't even that surprised, because someone that led women in prayer and worshiped extraordinary objects couldn't be an ordinary person. I tried to follow his finger, but it didn't satisfy him. He didn't believe me. He kept asking if I could see. I nodded, but evidently I wasn't convincing, because in the end he exclaimed: "Not there, over there! Over there!" A moment later he realized why I was having trouble. He pulled me to him abruptly and picked me up. It was only now that I could see a distant, thin strip of land. My eyes strayed along the livid line, and finally, at the end, encountered the outline of a church steeple like a sharpened pencil. It was barely there, no different in color than the indistinct ribbon of the horizon. "There?" I asked. "There," he replied. "That was where I received holy baptism," he added emphatically. After a long pause, as if he wanted to reward me, do something special for me, he added almost cheerfully, "They took me there by boat."

For a long time I was unable to free myself of that image: Two people I didn't know climb into a boat. They're poor, but dressed up. The man is in a dark ill-fitting jacket and a white shirt fastened at the neck. He smells of mothballs. The woman's wearing a simple dress the color of photographic sepia. She has a headscarf on. She's carrying a bundle in her arms. The boat pitches. The woman is frightened. The man reassures her and tells her to sit down on the narrow bench. He himself takes up a long oar with a metal fitting at the end and pushes off from the shore. They're both barefoot. Their shoes are placed on the bench next to the woman. The boat leaks. It's possible the man takes off his jacket. It's hot. The sun is shining directly overhead. Their bank soon becomes as distant as the one they're heading for. In the middle of the water they can scarcely be seen. The woman is increasingly afraid, because she's never been so far away from the whole world in all her life. In fact, her fear is twofold. And the man knows she's frightened, but he's also aware that on this occasion he can't tell her off, so he merely repeats that it's not far now. He too is anxious in a way he's never felt before. He bends low and immerses the oar all the way up to the crosspiece at the end of the handle, but he's still out of his depth and has to row with a narrow blade meant only for shallow water. For eternally long moments they're lonelier than they've ever been before, and probably than they'll ever be again. He stands behind her and can see only her back and her arms, curled in their embrace. The woman lacks the courage to shift or turn around. Her lips move soundlessly. When they find themselves in the middle of the current, the space around them becomes still and they're sure they will never reach the other side, though there are already dark patches on the man's white shirt. When the prow of the boat finally pushes in among the bulrushes they can't believe it. On their return journey they have one less anxiety. The child is baptized now and in much less danger. The sun has swung to the west and to their left they're accompanied by their shadows.

As we crossed back over the island I asked my grandfather why they'd rowed across the river since the church was on the same side. True, it was six miles away, but it was on solid ground and a regular road led to it. "I don't know," he said. "Maybe they didn't have a horse and it was quicker by water. In those days a lot of children died and people were afraid. Everyone was in a hurry."

We made it over the Break in a few minutes. It grew tiny. We'd barely pushed off and already we were at the other side. The cows of the entire village had gathered along the bank. Some of them were in up to their knees, drinking. Along with ooze, fish, and willows, that was a fourth smell to the half lifeless water: cows. The smell of milk, warm animal hair, and greenish cowshit. They stood there in the shallows with their tails raised releasing watery streams that splashed into the river. They were being minded by an old guy who was known as "the Shepherd." He'd take turns eating in each of the homes in the village. I don't know if he got any money for what he did. It didn't look like he needed any. Plus, his bizarre, ragged outfit may not even have had pockets. He carried a stick and wore a hooded cloak that he never took off even in the hottest weather. At dawn he'd collect the cattle from the farmyards, then bring them back in the evening. He'd lead the herd through the village and each cow would unfailingly find its own farm. You only had to leave the gate open. The same in the morning, they'd join the procession without being told, lowing to one another. They were like a slow living pendulum that moved along the fences twice a day, there and back again, measuring out time in the village. A clock made of flesh, a mechanism of blood and bone, indolent, straggling, but inexorable. No one paid any heed to the ticking and chiming of the longcase clock in the dark living room, though my grandfather wound it up daily with a special key. Perhaps he just regarded it as another head of livestock that needed regular care, while the hours it rang were quite unconnected with actual time and were simply a folly, a whim, an extravagance, like the Pionier radio that played Stenia Kozłowska songs from the capital.

When we got out of the boat, my grandfather found his own cows among the dozens that were there. He went up, checked them over, and said something I didn't catch. He didn't so much as glance at the Shepherd.

And now, on this late April afternoon in Żmigród, I was a grown-up and I could do what I pleased. I went to the square near the post office. It was deserted. The merchants had gone. They'd taken away the scaffolding where they hung their colorful electrostatic wares. When the wind blew, sparks would crackle in among the blouses and shirts. The shiny multicolored garments would fill with air; women would touch the phantoms, taking the fabric between their fingers, rubbing it with knowing pleasure and admiration, imagining their own bodies in place of the air. Yellow, orange, pink; gold buttons, frills, plastic brooches, chains, flounces, red lacquer, the fragile tinplate of buckles, stilettos with pointed toes and heels narrow as an umbrella ferrule, frothy jabots, shadowy low-cut necklines, the flora and fauna of appliqués, glassy markings of sequins, the polymeric sheen of lizard-pattern Lycra and the entomological transparency of puffy nylons with their pyrogenic lacework, stars, distant lands, wistful planetaria, the luciferic fictions of knitwear, moon-shaped clip-on earrings, knickknacks with holes, snakeskin, hairclips aspiring to be suns.

All this put me in mind of my grandfather's litany. As he kneeled amid the paper flowers, his body would gradually free itself of the torment of constant movement, the miracle-working pictures would unbind it and the mind turn flesh into light, while the "golden home" enclosed him in its walls and bore him to a space beyond the village, beyond the world, where reality became transformed, as did the torments of everyday life, even his membership of the volunteer fire brigade and his position as village chairman. It's entirely possible he found himself there with the whole village, all his worldly belongings, the stretch of pine grove he owned, his "crazy sons" as he called my uncles, and everything else in the world, including the firehouse and the squire's old mansion; *The Paris Commune* may also have been similarly favored, because, after all, matter is indivisible and when you agree to *A* you can't thumb your nose at *B*.

So then, as I stood there in Żmigród imagining the clothes market from that morning, I could see my grandfather relishing the successive invocations, the same way the women on the square had relished the marvelous outfits on sale that were magically imbued with their dreams of respite, of a sudden change of fate, a miracle of light, purity, of a shining that would heal, elevate, soothe their sad bodies that were locked in a desperate cycle of actions, of the beginning of one and the end of another, an end that was nowhere in sight.

At number two on the market square in Dukla there was a general store with a display window the size of a ticket window at a small train station. Generic herbal shampoo, green combs, Ludwik dish detergent, suntan lotion, sashes of linen rags, pink sponges, plain wire hairpins, a gold plastic openwork wastebasket, a pale blue china rabbit with a sugar bowl on its back, and three tattered rolls of toilet paper stacked in a pyramid. There's no accompanying sign, the things are what they are. They're fading in the sunlight since the window faces south. They're getting old, because the business has few customers. People prefer to visit actual stores rather than a place that looks like their own home.

This was later, in the summer. I was standing staring at this bizarre display, while my shadow lay half on the ground and half against the wall. The banal objects in the window suddenly took on the kind of significance the surrealists always dreamed of. The lack of a shop sign and the absence of any inscription left them utterly orphaned by everydayness. They were tragic caricatures. I lacked the courage to enter and look the heroic proprietor in the face. It was as if in this place the world had stopped flowing, as if it had frozen so as to show the meaning of immobilized change, the cruelty of a present strung between the desire for tomorrow and the possibility of yesterday. It was like makeup on a sixty-year-old woman, or a senior citizens' soccer match, or an old automobile proudly driving along under its own steam, unaware it's being taken to the junkyard.

And as I stood there with the sun at my back, I remembered our dog Blackie, who was already blind and deaf, and barely knew who we were; one day he disappeared, vanished somewhere, and though we looked for him for days we never found him, it was as if he'd wanted to leave us the hope that he'd simply gone away, the same way he'd just appeared one day ten or fifteen years earlier. And I thought to myself that if animals ever invented a religion, they would worship pure space, just as our own madness constantly revolves around time.

So it was summer already, and Dukla again, though this time I'd come in from the south. We'd spent two days visiting the Spiš region of Slovakia. The blueish heat eased a little in the valleys, but whenever the road climbed higher onto the vast languid mountain ridges with no shade, it resumed its glassy structure and far into the distance you could see successive hills swathed in hazy golden cornfields with the red bugs of distant combine harvesters as if in a collectivized land of plenty, because the whole was completely undivided by any field boundaries or country roads, nothing but gold down below, azure up above, and blue road signs with the names of the towns and villages.

In the late afternoon we parked on the market square in Podolínec along with four other cars, all old. The houses had been where they were for two or three hundred years. The few people around all resembled each other. Two Gypsies followed us with their eyes, then returned to their cigarettes and their silence. There were two or three others with them. One was pushing a moped loaded with mown grass. We passed him on the long street that runs by the square. There was nothing but barns along it. Large, ramshackle, their gables pointing toward the road. There was also a flock of white turkeys. Aside from the moped there wasn't a living soul, not a creak, not the trace of a sound, only buildings. We could feel a kind of presence, but it was somehow diluted. In places there was some movement far down an alley, something was happening, but it was too little for a sizeable town. A kind of timelessness hung over everything. M. told me afterward she'd found it the kind of place you'd want to stay in forever, without giving any particular reason, while I thought to myself that there are places where everything we've been up to the present moment is gently and profoundly brought into question, and we feel a bit like, say, a bird that suddenly realizes it has no air under its wings, but instead of disaster we find ourselves facing an endlessly long rest, a boundless soft falling. That was how it was in Podolínec. It looked like a town whose supply of things to happen had run out. Even C. kept talking only about the past, though the whole way there he'd been wrapped up in practical romantic plans.

But in the end we drove on, because we wanted to get something to drink before nightfall. Though it may also have been a self-protective reflex, a fear that our life would start mocking its own more or less established forms.

We were saved by Spišská Belá. We found something there that was half alleyway, half tiny market square where women perched on the steps in front of their houses and watched their menfolk, who were sitting on benches a few yards way in the dark blue late afternoon shade, drinking Smädný Mních or ordinary Šariš out of green bottles. Close by, in the corner building there was a little store. Inside, the place had a hazy yellow glow, rather like in a dream, mysterious, as if from some other time, from before the war, but all the things in there were real. They had tar-black Fernet, and Velkopopovický, though only the No. 10, and Chesterfields in the short Slovak version.

We kept driving and driving, but the day wouldn't end. In the small towns, between the walls, it was already late, but the moment we found ourselves out in open country the light gained in strength. Architecture and geography were playing mental blindman's buff with us.

Along the road to Kežmarok, Gypsies had taken up residence in the middle of nowhere. All around, as far as the eye could see there were miles and miles of meadows, while somewhere in their imagined middle was a lone concrete block. Nothing more, just that: gray, angular, crumbling. Dark-skinned children gave us a friendly wave. Guys were standing around in groups, laundry was drying, and you could see there was an atmosphere of calm unconstraint peculiar to people accustomed to waiting. They'd commandeered this chunky Corbusieresque piece of work and thereby lessened its ugliness, because they'd caused it to lose all signs of permanence. Neglected, dirty, hung about with rags, surrounded by shacks and junk, it was slowly turning into something mineral and subject to erosion. In this way a creation of high civilization had been occupied by a distant archaic tribe solely so it could be returned to the indifferent world of nature.

Then there was Kežmarok. It had the obligatory stork's nest on a tall chimney, alleyways, and little apartment houses with façades that C. knew a lot about, while I saw in them only various stages of decay: ongoing, arrested, or past continuous, temporarily turned back by the hands of painters and stucco-workers.

We had garlic soup at an outdoor restaurant where there were soldiers in green fatigues. Alas, they weren't drunk and they were not singing. They looked more like underage drinkers enjoying an illicit beer. They seemed like a very tranquil sort of army, I thought. After all, they'd never won or lost any war. After the soup we ordered sausage, because C. really took a shine to the waitress and he kept wanting to order something else, he kept forgetting something or other, and after his third beer we had to remind him he was driving. He agreed with us completely, and as a compromise, for the fourth round he only ordered a small one. We waited for dusk to fall over Kežmarok, so everything around us would disappear and there'd be darkness, which is the same everywhere, and allows you to breathe freely.

The next day we went to Levoča, because someone had told us the food was good at U Troch Apoštolov, but the place was too stuffy-smart so we went to Janus's on Kláštorská. The people at the tables looked like hyperreal portraits. It was brighter than in Poland at the same hour. The woman at the next table lit a cigarette but I didn't see the flame, just the smoke, all at once. We'd crossed the Carpathians, fled their northern shadow, and all of a sudden light was omnipresent. It emerged from the walls, the sky, the pavement, as if the sun had lost its monopoly and now the objects newly liberated from it were producing their own light, or at least trying to store it up. The dumplings, gravy, potatoes, sausage, and cabbage still belonged to the north, but everything else was more like fire than earth. The sulfurous yellow walls of the buildings, the red and orange and pink of flowers in the window boxes of crumbling apartment houses on Vysoká, sweat and suntan, the tedium of the bluish void with the livid Poprad highway like a dead snake lying belly-up, and the bar with no sign where dark-skinned, tattooed men in T-shirts sat drinking Šariš beer and flipping the levers of a pinball machine, and the only woman was a pale, skinny barmaid. A bit farther on, sitting on some steps was another girl, swarthy, dark-eyed, with dyed blonde hair. She was holding a baby, while next to her lay a pack of LMs, and when we came back the same way an hour later nothing had changed except the pack of cigarettes was almost empty, and that was exactly what afternoons looked like on Vysoká Street. Afternoons on the south side of town, on the sun-scorched, burned-out slopes that dropped toward Levočsky Creek, with the yellow houses that looked frail and flammable, and even though they were built of stone, and even though they were handsome, you couldn't help feeling they were temporary, that they'd been temporary for three hundred years, because they lacked the definitive weightiness of buildings in the north, where they constitute one's sole, indispensable shelter.

We turned into Žiacka; here it was siesta time. The Gypsies gave us unfriendly stares, though we weren't so different from them. We were poor too, and we too were killing time. They were sitting on walls, steps, benches, listening to their music on tape players. The glare of the sun settled on their bodies and disappeared. They were like ripe fruit. Laborers were demolishing a house on the corner, but the Gypsies didn't even look at them. Right nearby someone's world was coming to an end and it didn't bother them in the slightest. The music drowned out the din of collapsing walls. The afternoon's vertical white dazzle blurred the shadows, and Žiacka looked like the alleyway of eternity, or an icon.

We went to St. James's. The famous altarpiece by Master Pavol of Levoča was decidedly too small. The doll-like Gothic looked as though it had only just gone on display. People were wandering in every direction, craning their necks. For two korunas you could listen to a history talk from a metal cabinet. I was drawn to the confessionals, though: both confessor and penitent could enclose themselves in a huge wooden chest. Not like in Poland, where the sinner has to kneel before the eyes of the entire church, his only thought how to rise as quickly as possible and melt back into the throng of decent folk.

From St. James's we walked down Sirotínska toward the city walls, then to the Franciscan monastery. The shadows of the stone building were cool and deserted. We saw an old woman squatting against the wall of the church and peeing. We slowed down to give her time. She unhurriedly pulled up her stout pink underwear and let down her skirt. She was wearing a headscarf. She didn't look at us but simply disappeared around the corner. A minute later we saw her inside the half-empty church, joining the old ladies sitting in the pews. They were reciting a litany to the Holy Spirit. Our new acquaintance had slipped out between the first invocation and the second, and now she resumed her place. She reminded me of the women who used to gather in my grandfather's house on Sundays, then trek over to the church four miles away. The sandy road led through pinewoods. It was hot, dust would be hanging in the air. The horses would be plodding quietly and heavily in their harnesses. Their sweating black and bay rumps glistened in the sun. The women would occasionally take a seat in one of the wagons, but mostly they'd walk. They'd carry their plain black sandals with low heels and their patent leather handbags where they had prayer books with large clear print. Their step was like the step of the horses: lengthy, tense, strong. They sank up to their ankles in the sand. From time to time one of them would lean her hand on the side of a wagon to take a rest, still walking, the way a swimmer rests at the side of a boat. They didn't perspire. They walked quickly, leaning forward, as though the road led into the wind, and they had strength enough to join in groups and talk. They joked, bantered, and the gold and silver of their teeth flashed with a childlike playfulness. Dust settled on their brown feet. After the hard uneven ground of farmyards and prickly stubble fields, the soft warm path was a relief. They only put their shoes on in front of the church. The more fastidious ones took out a handkerchief and hastily wiped the dust from their feet and calves. Some went in the bushes and peed almost standing, hiking up their Sunday dresses. The horses cooled off in the shade while the men slung nosebags around their necks. The scents of animals and humans mingled over the sun-heated square. Powerful streams of horse urine frothed like beer and instantly soaked into the ground. The smell of sweat-soaked harness straps, horse farts, cigarettes, and soap melted into one, as if Sunday were both a human and an animal holiday. The weather descended upon the church square like an indifferent grace. The girl from next door was wearing a grown-up dress in place of her skimpy red outfit. She looked like the other women and was of no interest.

Some time after that, we talked for the first time. I met her on top of a sand dune that separated the village from the river. She sat down next to me and toyed with some broken shells. Her skinny brown body never ceased to be in motion. She slipped her bare feet into the sand as if it were bedding, built a mound around them, dug them out again, then started making a deep hole. Her arm, which was like a smooth thin tree branch, bore into the ground all the way to the compact layer of wet earth. She told me about how one boy had cut his leg with a scythe down to the bone; he ran here, buried his leg in the sand, and when he took it out it was healed, without any trace of a wound. "The earth can heal anything," she said. "Even lightning, even then you can bury whoever it is and afterward they'll get up like nothing ever happened." She sat there plunged up to her hips in a wave of loose sand, and it seemed as if she was sinking deeper and deeper. She looked like one of those gypsy dolls they put on the top of a pile of bedding during the day, except that instead of spread skirts she had sand, an entire hill of sand all the way to the riverbank. But it only lasted a moment, because she soon broke free of her new garment, knelt, rocked back on her heels and asked in an intent, lowered voice: "Did you know that when you go into a Baptist church you have to spit on the cross and step on it?" I didn't know what Baptists were. She didn't either, but fear had settled between us, the sky darkened, and I suddenly smelled the heat of her perspiration. "Don't look at me like that, it's true," she said. She began poking about in the sand around herself. She found two sticks, made a cross with them and laid them on the ground between us. "So are you afraid?" she asked, while I sat at the ready like a dog, gripping handfuls of sand in my fists. At that moment a ball of saliva emerged from her mouth; just before it landed it swelled into a bubble. Then she jumped to her feet and finished the job with a bare heel. She burst into giggles and kneeled abruptly. She whispered right into my face: "But that doesn't count, it wasn't real, you know? It wasn't from a church, it wasn't blessed. It's gone, see?" She scattered sand every which way. "See? There's nothing there!" She got up, brushed off her hands and knees and looked down at me. I could only see her silhouette. "If you tell anyone I'll say you did it too, I'll say it was your idea."

And so things remained between us. We'd meet from time to time, but she was always aloof and indifferent. It was as if she had some power over me. I watched her from afar, running across her farmyard, feeding the chickens, carrying pails of water and snapping back at her mother; she was dark-skinned and angular as a boy, set apart from everyday reality, untouchable.

From Levoča we went to Spišský Hrad, but the castle was too big, and the space around it too vast, to be able to even think about it. C. drove fast, so as to finally put behind him all those Slovakian wonders that had played such havoc with our minds, all the way down to the bare bone of our skulls. Široké, Prešov, and the whole of Spiš were suddenly behind us, along with all the renaissance façades of churches, which somewhere beyond Kapušany yielded to the flat roofs of collective-farm architecture, while the storks' nests were replaced by loudspeakers mounted on telegraph poles. In Svidník, not far from an insane church shaped like a flying saucer, we returned our empty Kozel bottles and got a few full ones so as not to reenter Poland like total tourists. A few miles further on it already felt like home. Along the highway, various military objects were arrayed on dressed stone plinths. There was a cannon, a Soviet fighter plane, and a good old teddy-bear-like T-34. One particularly huge monument depicted a fascist Tiger tank being crushed under the wheels of a Soviet vehicle. The place smelled of Dukla and of Poland.

III.

to the memory of Z. H.

And here I am again. The sky has a milky color and more and more people are arriving. They're coming down Zielona, 3 Maja, Mickiewicza, and Sawickiej, they're approaching on Węgierski

Trakt, Żwirki, and Cergowska. The women are carrying plastic bags. They're wearing knee-length stockings, flip-flops, or sandals. They climb out of buses, press together in tightly packed herds, they move toward the market square and it's only there that they get their courage back, because after all it's a village and it looks like the other villages they've come from. It's going to rain. The light is barely able to filter through the air. Shadows are faint. The world is hopelessly old. Stall owners are spreading out their wares. Outside Mary Magdalene you can buy fluorescent rosaries, glow-in-the-dark Our Ladys, and Egyptian dream books, while meat is being grilled on Parkowa. There's no wind. Traffic is slow. The bed of the Dukielka has been lined with rocks, but beyond the dam it flows the way it always used to. It smells of slow-moving water, decay, mud. The day is slipping across the surface of time. A tiny old lady in black is examining Blessed Johns in different poses. They're lined up on a laminated plastic tabletop. They're watched over by a guy with a cigarette and signet rings. Big ones are a hundred, little ones eighty, they're all brown, there must be a good forty of them, and they're still warm. The world is getting old and things are growing indistinct and imprecise. Soon they'll all become indistinguishable and that'll be the end of it. Only designations will be left.

Outside the monastery, police uniforms intermingle with monks' habits. The monks are clean-shaven. The police officers have mustaches. The heat embraces them all and holds them to its sticky belly. In the park it's still cool. Three men are drinking wine there. They must have bought it yesterday, or today under the counter. As usual they're smoking. The viscid water offers no reflections. Bicycle-tire tracks can be seen in the dark mud along the linden-lined path. People swing by here to take a leak. It's a good place. Couples holding hands disappear into the bushes. The trees are marked with the dull-colored trails of Roman snails. It's all going to happen on the far side of Węgierski Trakt, on the cemetery hill. Wooden fences divide the loamy slope into sectors. Hardly anyone is there yet. Clouds drift over the cemetery, vanish in some imperceptible fashion, and reappear goodness knows how. It's as if they're rising out of the depths of the sky. Guys swing by the tourist office bar without any special hope, and the barmaid shrugs helplessly—no alcohol sales today. The out-of-towners are drinking tea and eating egg sandwiches. Loudspeakers outside the monastery announce that "today, the whole world is watching our little Dukla." The garbage men have new green overalls and a smart-looking truck. They're standing by the ruins of the synagogue, which has been made into a repository for old curbstones and paving slabs. Children weave by on bicycles, and the new café in the town hall is serving Lavazza coffee with a free cookie. Everything is supposedly as it used to be. Small streams of visitors fall still about the town, looking like ornaments. Sizzling kebabs, hamburgers, soda machines stocked with Coke and Sprite, coaches, a whole array of license plates, cordons, ten new phone booths that take phone cards, red paving stones, banners and flags—it all gives off the sad smell of humanity. It's proved impossible to demolish Dukla and build it again anew.

So here I am again. It's raining. People scurry by in transparent raincoats. The guys from the gas company are sitting in their van playing blackjack. I came early in the morning so as to observe it all. Now I'm sitting in my car listening to news from the outside world. It's raining elsewhere in Poland too. I couldn't resist. Things ought to end somehow or other. Like breakfast, a book, cigarettes. Pilgrims with umbrellas are carrying folding chairs. The flags hang vertically. The locals look like outsiders. The plastic bottles of mineral water have a gray-blue sheen. It all must be heading in a particular direction, like the blood in our bodies, like the air there, like all of the physiology that allows us to see everything and smell things. A white Hungarian truck moves cautiously among the pedestrians. The driver honks his horn. They look at him like he's an intruder. In the store at the bus station they buy bread, cheese, canned goods. They're dressed a little like boy scouts, a little like old-time tourists, and a little like they're just going for an after-dinner constitutional. The paradoxical boundary between adventure and everydayness. Camouflage jackets, backpacks, Sunday-best handbags, high heels, hunting knives dangling from belts, idiot-proof cameras that cost eight hundred at the toy store. Every second person has one. Outside the jeweler's some guy has set up a stall selling film. Now he puts up a plastic awning and continues doing business. Yellow Kodak and green Fuji. Reality freezing in hundreds of sequences, thousands of split-second incarnations. I try to imagine the world before photography and I fail. It probably never really existed, it continually kept disappearing, swallowed up by unsated senses forever in motion, and nothing remained. Whereas now, the untold numbers of clicks, the mosaic, second after second, look after look, mom, dad, son, everyone making irreversible choices with their fingers, and if you try really hard not even a single drop of rain will escape, vanish, return where it came from. It's entirely possible there'll come a time when the whole world, and all time, will be reconstructed on the basis of compounds of silver. Frame by frame, roll by roll; and it's entirely possible that this will be the only fulfillment and only end.

After an hour or so it stops raining and people can come out again. Outside Mary Magdalene there's a cardboard sign reading "Tickets for Dukla." I pay one zloty and get Sector B2, but there's still time, so I wander off to the mansion. My 150 is parked on the grounds next to a rusting abandoned greenhouse. Both objects look equally unnecessary. I walk about and watch people. They all look like my grandfather, my grandmother, my mother, my father, like all the people I've known and seen in my life. Their shoes pinch, they limp, they sweat in their wrinkle-proof outfits, and examine the goods for sale at the stalls, medallions, white busts, colored prints, canvas beach chairs for four fifty; they sniff at the food on the grills, chicken breasts, sausage, bacon, dark glistening blood pudding. From time to time the sun comes out and captures their silhouettes in misty aureoles. Busy with their ice creams, Pepsis, mineral water, and children, they fail to notice this indifferent caress. They enter the strip of shade in the park and pass between a double row of firefighters toward the monastery. There, in place of my spurned cannon there now stands the figure of Blessed John. "He's kind of all ragged," says a girl with a video camera, and pans across the brown sculpture. Then she films a macabre cross with dozens of severed hands jutting from its base.

But the cannon really was better—like anything, incidentally, that has no desire to be more than it actually is. Church dignitaries in snazzy cassocks emerge from a dark blue limousine. Sweat stains start to appear on the cops' uniform shirts. A row of confessionals has been set up on the cemetery hill. People form lines. Then they line up for the brightly colored portable toilets. Three confessionals and three lavatories. Dark brown, yellow, light blue, and red. Except for the people in line, everyone looks like they're just out for a stroll. They go as far as they can, turn back and return to town, then after a while they repeat the exercise. The day is passing quietly and monotonously. A chemical suspension of wet heat lifts bodies up like objects. It's like a festival of presence, a parade about how to fill space, a display of ways to prove one's existence. The bodies rub against each other, touch, join scents and thermic auras. The immense aquarium of the afternoon has its end somewhere beyond what is imagined, and if anyone's watching us they must be feeling pity. After all, the only thing we've come up with to counter unbounded space is the ability to assemble, to gather together, to occupy the smallest possible area. So as to sense through our skin the existence of others, since we're uncertain of our own. A police Land Rover from Ustrzyki pulls up in front of the monastery. The unusual nature of this day has the taste of concentrated ordinariness. It's like perfume—we only become aware of it when there's a lot of it. Someone's filming the empty Krosno road as if empirically documenting a miracle. Light enters deep into the apparatus and dies there, just as images die inside our skulls, then later serve as excuses, justifications, explanations for any occasion. While they're still alive there's nothing we can do with them.

It's only once they become things that we know more or less how to make use of them. Now a Land Rover from Jasło appears, and an ordinary police Polonez with a silent siren on its roof.

Actually, I'm not doing anything other than describing my own physiology. Changes in the magnetic field recorded by my retina, fluctuations in temperature, differing concentrations of scent particles in the air, oscillations of sound frequencies. That's what the world is composed of. The rest is formalized madness or the history of humanity. And as I stand here across from the post office in Dukla, smoking and watching heavyset guys in shiny boots, it occurs to me that existence has to be a fiction if we're to have the slightest chance. That flesh, blood, light, and everything else that's self-evident has to turn out one day to be merely a curious illusion, because otherwise something just isn't right and it's goodbye Norma Jean, thanks but no thanks, we open again at 1:00 P.M. tomorrow. This is precisely the naïve thought that comes to me now in Dukla, whose stillness makes it possible to daydream about how things might be. Magic lantern, camera obscura, a crystal ball in which snow gently falls, a slide sequence of last hopes, a metaphysical peep show.

The tiny old lady in black appears now here, now there. She's alone and alert. She stares at the town as if seeing it for the first time, though she's from here. The world has suddenly come to her and it's like a journey to distant lands, with all these bishops, habits, gleaming limousines, flags, choirs singing over loudspeakers, prelates, sidewalks of new red brick. It's a sudden, overnight materialization of holiness, a little as if she were moving around in paradise, like a child in a toy store, like a prisoner on his first day of freedom, or a bride in her wedding dress. She's wearing small men's shoes with a polished black sheen. She pauses here and there, tiny as a little girl and just as timid, trying to see something through the throng of idling, inquisitive, self-confident onlookers. She resembles a little black bird or a character from a fairy tale. Her arms are folded on her stomach and pressed to her body as though she were striving to occupy as little room as possible. Some young monks scuttle past with a swish of their habits. To move even faster they hike them up and you can see their trousers. Their faces are like the faces of young professionals in the city. One of them is carrying a Yamaha keyboard, another a stylish attaché case with a digital lock. The faces of the firefighters, on the other hand, are from early Forman. When I was here two years ago they were marching in a funeral procession. Now they stand in their cordon and look on helplessly as the crowd seeps through the uneven dark blue chain of their uniforms. From time to time they spread their arms as if they were trying to embrace someone, but these are only gestures of resignation, and to save face they light cigarettes and wait till the cops come to their rescue.

One adolescent girl with a completely shaved head is wearing a T-shirt that says in English: "I hate religion." The word "religion" appears right over her small breasts. In this crowd of fathers with children, women with handbags, couples in white socks and flip-flops, her figure is just as small and helpless as the old lady in black.

The jingling things around her neck, her Doc Martens, and the stubborn gravity of her sixteen years swathes her existence here in an extraordinarily beautiful melancholy. She walks along the wall of the park as though naked, yet no one pays any attention to her.

Two guys in jackets are sitting on a wire cage containing pigeons, under a tree. They're smoking Popularnys, chatting, passing a bottle of Wysowianka mineral water back and forth. The bottle shuttles between them, and each time before they drink they raise the plastic container as if they're toasting one another. A matron in a pink dress and purple jacket is examining some white china busts. She picks each one up in turn, flips it over, weighs it in her hand, like she was looking for the heaviest. In the end she chooses one of many identical copies, pays, puts it in her shopping bag and says to the lady running the stall: "At last he's coming here as well. He'll clean out that Jewish stink."

There are also some plumpish girls with chunky calves. They have backpacks and knee-length camouflage pants, hiking boots, guitars, and large crosses on straps. They're looking for some shade so they can sit and sing a bit in a safe circle. Their short hair is stuck down with perspiration, and their blouses are dark and wet under the arms. They find a cool spot, take out some yellow sheets, and begin a song: "Model of life, teach us virtue each day. May caution bring light to our nation, and troubles not fall in our way."

Among people, among their bodies, the imagination dies away. They pass by like figures from sociology or psychology. Life takes on ready-made forms, reflecting and refracting light, and there's nothing I can do. Faces, arms, breasts, buttocks—my analysis is a complete disaster. Cigarettes, outfits, jewelry, high heels, lace ruffles, cell phones on belts, bangles, the poor life, cheap crap or wholesale stuff, houses, apartments, the Virgin Mary, crystal, gleaming shelves carrying *Chronicle of the Twentieth Century* imitation leather couches, ferns on windowsills, the smell of bedrooms, crystal-clear displays of time and function, air fresheners in johns, linoleum, a Sacred Heart in a rococo frame, a black Panasonic, "extended payment plan available," "St. Christopher, pray for us" by the rearview mirror, videotapes from the wedding, from the reception, videotapes from Spain, a crocheted doily on the record player, on that a glass dog, microwave oven, stove, rubber boots in the hallway, potatoes in a crate, baseball caps, earrings, Puma and Adidas knockoffs, alkaline batteries, a lightbulb in a lampshade made of newspaper, golden plastic ship's wheels with barometers in the middle, bare walls reflecting the sounds of the television and the shadows of distant events, the murmur and damp of new houses, "where did you put the car keys," Sunday, gleam of auto bodywork outside the church, bracelets, chains, Consul aftershave, Samson aftershave, Gillette antiperspirant, Spandex, calves, red fingernails, curls, pumps like Aldo Binets, pushed-up breasts, a curiosity shop of perfumes and accessories, old age, bone combs in gray buns, bamboo handles of square-cornered handbags, children washed and laundered and colorful, wedding rings permanently attached to arthritic fingers, men's bellies, pride, wristwatches, moccasins with tassels, solemnity, satiety, as it was in the beginning, is now, and forever will be, glamour, Moorish arches, a cow right outside, drywall, cheap Popularny cigarettes, porn, hymns, the Feast of

Our Lady's Assumption and of Our Lady of the Sowing, itsy-bitsy teeny-weeny tiny polka-dot bikini, Come Holy Spirit—the world is a counting rhyme. It can't be understood any other way, because things push between ideas and tear at their delicate edges with sharp corners, and everything that's general ends up on the trash heap, buried by details. *Caro salutis est cardo.*

So. I've come here again. This time in a twenty-year-old dark blue Mercedes. The police were already blocking the roads, but we stuck behind a blue Volkswagen with its siren blaring and we managed to sneak through. Now evening's falling and the light has turned golden and thick as blood. The towers of the Cistercian monastery are black. The red of the fire trucks has also dimmed. I look from the north to the south. To the right, over the cemetery the outline of a cloud is smoldering like a roll of paper. To the left is Cergowa Mountain, oozing darkness. The shadows dwell in the earth. They emerge out of it then return, like some immense breathing process. Children build a town from pebbles and empty bottles. They put up walls and raise towers. They make people out of sticks and refuse. Grown-ups cast long shadows over it all. They move, change place, shift about in the network of sectors enclosed by a double cordon of police. The men head for the nearby bushes. You can see their straightened backs against the wall of greenery. A six-foot-six photographer with a minute Leica on his chest is looking for praying crowds. A young priest has been standing by the barrier for several hours now. He hasn't moved an inch. He's holding a Praktica, aiming it down the dark maw of Węgierski Trakt. The boys spread out their jackets, the girls sit down. Couples stroll by. This is the young men's only entertainment—to watch the girls' swaying backsides and imagine a life together, conversations in the morning, apartments, dinner with the parents. Someone accidentally lets go of a red balloon. People stir for a few moments, till it disappears in the sky. A man in a beat-up motorcycle helmet has a big eagle on the back of his jacket, drawn in ballpoint pen. Its head is surrounded with a halo of glittering silver studs. The loudspeakers announce that Father Jankowski is here. Potbellied guys hold Klubowe cigarettes in huge hands and discuss who's going to get the wood from the barriers dividing the sectors. "You could come for it at night," one of them says. "It'll be lit up," says another. "Not tomorrow night, maybe." "You never know with those people." "It's good stuff. Four-inch. Be great for rafters." "Come off it—three-inch at the most." "That'd do too." They go take a look. There's not one single dog. That's why everything's so still, even though people are walking around, looking for good spots. They clamber up higher, then come down again so as to be closer, but down in the front are the toughest folks, packed tight in a long line, immovable.

On the far side of the cemetery hill a golden fire is crackling, but here it's already dark and cool. Figures lose their distinctness. They look like their own shadows. A portable radio is playing. Choirs sing in front of the monastery. Over there it's brighter. Blotches of light can be seen, and something's moving as though in a distant window. Some people tear their eyes from the highway and stare in that direction. They're reassured by the loudspeakers. Now we look older and we're all gradually starting to resemble one another. At dusk, space withers away, only time remains, and for that reason we huddle even closer together. Someone calls someone else's name. Fathers pick up their children. Blackness is approaching from the direction of Cergowa Mountain. The lights of cigarettes can be seen. Matches held in closed hands are like lanterns of pink skin.

I watched him from far off. He was white in the darkness, and barely moving. He was speaking to people who were walking away toward the town. His voice, magnified by the loudspeakers, was soft and frail. From that distance he resembled a baby bird in its nest. All around were shadows, only over there was the little patch of light. Night was beginning a few yards from him, and extending into infinity. People were going home to light their lamps and get something to eat. "I wish I'd gotten his autograph," said a girl in a leopard-skin pattern top to her boyfriend. Other people were walking behind them and were also talking. They were carrying sleeping children. There was a tapping of heels and the sound of air being displaced by their bodies. Dukla had never had as many pedestrians.

I had no wish to get closer. I mean, either way I wouldn't go up to him. Ordinary people didn't stand a chance, though it was probably for them that he'd come. But I wasn't interested in paradoxes. I was trying to think about immortality and I was thinking about his body, his figure, the way it had been shaped, his material form. I was imagining him waking in the morning and feeling a tiredness that sleep is incapable of dispelling. His bones, muscles, blood are leaden and will not obey him. More and more they're living their own life. This is a surrogate for proof of the existence of the soul—the awareness that our body is leaving us, moving away in its own direction. Waking, rising, bedroom slippers, the bathroom mirror and other objects no longer warm from their previous use. All human actions, eating, bread, tea, the everyday litany recreating life as such. I was imagining him without the crowd and without his robes. Alone, naked almost, in the wan light of early morning as he repeated the same movements as the rest of world at that time of day. He shaves, brushes his teeth, combs his hair, carefully measures out his sugar or goes without, just as he's cutting down on fatty foods, hard-to-digest meat and white bread, just as he cuts his movements down to an essential minimum, avoiding stairs, slippery floors, and poorly lit places where it's easy to trip. He guards himself from cold air, drafts, the sinusoidal curve of emotions, loud noise, sleeplessness, and bad news. I was imagining the moments in which he listened in silence to his own body.

I'm reminded of my grandmother, who believed in ghosts. She often saw them. My grandparents' house stood in an old orchard at the edge of the village. She'd tell about the things she saw in a completely calm, natural manner. They would appear both during the day and at night. They'd come into the kitchen, open the door just like that. They'd find her at her everyday chores in the kitchen or the farmyard. They were somewhat human, but made of a slightly airier substance. They usually looked like somebody from the family. Everyone believed these stories. I did too. It was true faith, because it was unsupported by any experience. Nor did it have anything to do with religion. In my grandmother's stories the world of supernatural beings didn't have anything to do with the world of the saints, the church, ritual. The former was an everyday matter, while the latter served as a measure of time, material for invocations and for a moment of respite on Sundays. The ghosts came as visible proof that in essence reality is indivisible, and that things are rather different than they appear. I was very fond of my grandmother. She was a mild-mannered, practical woman without a hint of excessive piousness, religiosity, without any inclination to mysticism. "He came in that way, he stood here, opened a drawer, the spoons rattled, but he left everything the way it was." I was captivated by this specificity. These events always had their own time and their own place. "At six in the morning, I'd just woken up and I was sitting on the bed. But he didn't come from the hallway, he came from the back room." Her reports were entirely disinterested. They weren't trying to prove anything or promise anything. To this day I believe them, and I've never since come across signs so plain and direct. The one concession to the miraculous that my grandmother would make would be to insert into her story an involuntary and rhetorical: "I really got a scare." But her fear wasn't actually visible. It sounded more like, "What a surprise," or, "How do you like that." Her friends and relatives were simply visiting her. They came from the past, stood a moment by the window or the white dresser, then went away, leaving behind them an open door that she had to shut herself, because there was a draft. Sometimes she'd even quote snippets of conversation, but I don't recall they ever said anything that might have confirmed the unusual nature of their condition. I imagined to myself that they were dull gray in color, that they were a little more transparent than people, that they had no smell and wore regular clothes. And that was probably how it was. Grandmother never actually described them. She only spoke about what they'd been doing, how they had occupied space and time with their presence that was somewhat beyond both time and space.

Later, my grandmother died. I woke up in the next room, and my aunts, who'd been watching over her, said: "Your grandmother's gone." I loved her and I was sad. She lay stretched out. Her face had suddenly become terribly serious and stern. I stood very close and gazed at her, in the quiet of the early morning I could hear my aunts bustling around behind my back as if it were just another ordinary morning in a house in the village, and I had the feeling that this death, and maybe death in general, was somehow, how shall I put it, overrated. I felt that my grandmother was only partially gone. I was certain she'd slipped out of this room and this world, but that she was somewhere very close by, that she'd simply gone among those who used to visit her, and if she only chose to she'd appear in just the same way they had appeared. In other words, I knew she was alive. She'd simply been unable to take her body, which now lay upon the bed. In all probability she hadn't needed it.

That was why I wasn't afraid. Neither then or later, when she was dressed in her Sunday best and laid in her casket, and I had to kiss her before the lid was closed. I felt foolish, because everyone was crying and I couldn't. I knew none of it was true. They couldn't have been listening to her carefully when she was alive. In the end I started crying too, but it was just because for the first time in my life I saw tears in my father's eyes.

It was only when the black mourning flag was stuck on the house that I felt true dread. It flapped in the autumn wind, and this was the breeze of truly dead death. I was utterly unable to connect this symbol to my grandmother's living presence. It was an abstraction, the horror of emptiness, the black hole of the liturgy and the nameless infinity of oblivion.

So. I'm standing by the park wall in Dukla and practicing the cult of the ancestors. I'm observing a hieratic ceremony taking place in the distance and trying to imagine my grandmother standing in this spot or a little farther off, by the post office, where the cordon begins and the guys in bulletproof vests are pacing back and forth. She always admired bishops and cardinals, but she saw their job as being entirely earthly, for example, appearing dignified and official. The world simply looked better when it had a prelate in it. She was never visited by saints, or priests, even though she'd outlived at least three of them in the village church. I think about her, her kind wrinkled face. The elderly women walking down the Trakt toward town multiply her image. Many of them have come from far away. They longed to behold his face, and now they're returning, satisfied and sated or disappointed. The most commonly heard words in the crowd are "did you see him," "I did," "other people got in the way," "just caught a glimpse," "we were too far away." They'd come to see his body, because that's something almost as sure as touch, which functions even in silence and darkness. Words belong to wiseacres and lazy insomniacs. We sniff at each other like animals. There's nothing wrong in this. It's better than nothing.

Beneath the horror-movie cross there's a group of young monks. They're touching the metal surface then rubbing their hands on their foreheads. They're touching the cross and transferring its blessing to their heads as if they could massage it into their skin, under their skulls, as if it could be captured, stored away, or grafted onto them. The sight is grotesque and barbaric. I really ought to laugh, but in fact I'm not doing anything all that different myself, except I'm keeping my hands discreetly in my pockets and only using my eyes. They're wearing sandals. They look as if they're washing themselves, or patting face cream on before going to bed. In essence, it's just a radical kind of photography, a sensual telepathy. That's why I don't even try to catch what they're saying, preferring to reflect on his body and on what connects us in a way that can't be undermined. We'll experience the same thing as everyone else. In the same air, the same space that took all those who came before us in its stride. The leaves beneath the streetlamps glisten and tremble like bunting. Stall owners are closing up shop. I'm sore from walking and from sitting now here, now there. Cops in field uniforms can be seen in the lighted windows of the school. They're lying on the tables resting. They smoke, flicking ash on the floor, and their lips are moving. His voice quavers, yet it rises and falls in calm cadences within an infinite solitude and bounces back off the dark hills. Cars turn on their lights and engines, inch through the crowd, speed up at the town limits, and disappear into the gloaming like red sparks. Everything has already happened. The space has swallowed up sounds and gestures. It's closed in, grown over without a trace, the same way it's closed in and grown over at every moment since the very beginning, and there'll be enough of it for everyone till the very end. The charcoal in the grills by Parkowa Street burn their last in the warm dark air. Girls in white aprons put leftover potatoes into crates. A short guy is counting the day's take beneath a yellow lightbulb. Tens, twenties, fifties, each separately. He thrusts the wads of money into the pocket of his sportsman's waistcoat and into a shopkeeper's pouch hanging from his belt. Two firefighters are eating the last kielbasa. One of them holds a lit cigarette in his free hand. There were no beggars today, nor probably any thieves.

I drink coffee from a small white mug and watch the rhythm of the story fading away. It's all over now. Doors close and lights go out. Tomorrow it'll be like nothing ever happened. There'll just be ten new blue public phones, and a red walkway. The men will sit themselves back down in the tourist office bar, at the Graniczna, the Gumisia. When it comes down to it, events differ only slightly from the moments they take place in. Even when you know where they've come from, it's hard to say where they're going. New ones constantly have to be made.

That evening, or night really, I went into Mary Magdalene. It was open, deserted, and only dimly lit. Amalia lay in shadow. The mirrors caught the dull glow of the streetlamps, but for some strange reason they failed to pass it on into the interior of the chapel. It remained in their silvery surfaces, heating them up coldly, without making anything brighter. Quite the opposite: the gloom intensified, congealing above the supine figure, entering into her fanciful marble gown, seeping in deeper and deeper and assuming the contours of her sleeping body. It was as dark and stuffy as in a bedroom. The foliage outside the window was in subtle motion, making the shadows restless. Flakes of semidarkness were trembling, spinning, flickering like will-o'-the-wisps between the relative brightness of the mirrors and the deep black of the air. There was no one around. From time to time a stray car headlight passed across the windows of the chapel and the place was enlivened with a dead, hyperreal clarity.

There inside were her remains, and they were occupying my thoughts: dust at the bottom of the black sarcophagus, a handful of phosphorizing minerals, calcium, salt, potassium, basic elements, and the remains of the lace in which she had walked about while she was still alive, and in which she'd been buried. Now it all took the form of a dry powdery substance only a little heavier than air, a substance that was almost spiritlike, because the wind could whip it away like an apparition, like the transparent contour of who knew what.

I tried to see my reflection in the mirrors. It wasn't there. All that could be seen were snatches of shadow, different kinds of darkness, airy phantoms. And then I heard a rustle and I saw Amalia sit up on her bed. I felt the air move, and a warm smell penetrated the ancient aroma of the church. She stretched. Her cap fell off and her long hair spilled onto her shoulders. She tossed it back, leaned her hands on the edge of the bedding, and turned her face toward the narrow window where the glow of the special day was fading. I wanted to say something, but I had the impression she couldn't see me. Occupied with herself, still sleepy, she was gradually fixing her outline in the depths of the June night— her magnetic skeleton attracting elementary particles out of the surrounding space and reassembling her body of old. People in Dukla and in the world beyond were falling asleep, slipping between the sheets and tumbling to the bottom of time, while she was emerging out of it, sitting on its rim listening intently to the rising pulse of her blood, the thickening warmth of matter, from her small feet, up her calves, thighs, through the middle of her belly and her spreading arms, right to the top of her head. Everything I had seen in life, everything others had seen, was entering into her and assuming shape. She was growing, acquiring strength, taking on substance and heat like the physical form of an obsessive thought or the answer to the oldest question. She was swelling with the deepest-held suspicions. They gave her an ideal, complete form, into which one could enter without leaving a trace. She was like a black sky poised over the earth, where space ceases to exist and all sounds fall silent. A resurrection has to consist of something. It was like air that had attained the density of flesh. All the dead, all things that have passed forever, the lost and gone shards of the world, parings of time, once-upon-a-time views from windows, everything that once was and will never be again, was now being transformed into her body. Death was withdrawing, pulling back like a glove, like the cracked casing of the everyday, and there, underneath, inside, memory and hope, imagination, and all the other weightless, invisible, and nonexistent phenomena were solidifying into living, palpable particles. Amalia was not a ghost or a phantom. She was the condensed presence of that which was always absent. She was a picture that was moving back toward its model so as to exceed it. The shoe slipped from her foot and fell to the floor with a thud. I could hear her breathing, hear the illusory matter of the world entering into her and being turned into flesh as soft and smooth as eternity. She excited desire. I could smell her scent: heavy, solid, firm. It touched me from every side, the way thought can touch an object—without either tenderness or cruelty, with the indifferent graciousness of inexhaustible things. Her skin glistened in the dark. It recalled the damp stone that formed the arcs of her shoulders, hips, thighs. Dukla was ceasing to exist beyond the wall. It had entered into her along with all the other events I'd lived through; I watched as they moved away one by one to their tranquil annihilation. And at no point did I ever think of a way to revive them, none except memory—that bastard of time over which no one ever has any power.

I took a step forward. I wasn't afraid. After all, it's hard to fear something that doesn't know you exist. My fingers in my pocket could feel a pack of cigarettes and some warm coins.

At that moment I heard a rustle from the direction of the vestibule. A slight figure appeared out of the shadows. It was the shaven-headed girl with the slogan on her T-shirt. She was carrying a small backpack. She passed by going down the nave, but I must have moved, because she noticed me and turned around. This time she was wearing an army jacket with a turned-up collar.

"I didn't think anyone was here," she said softly.

"Actually, there really isn't," I answered. "I was just leaving."

"Wonder if they lock the place at night," she said more loudly, in an artificially casual voice.

"I don't know. Probably."

"I was going to get some sleep. I've missed the Krosno bus for today. It's a bit scary to sleep in the park, and the town's crawling with cops." She went up to the last pew, slid into it and disappeared from view. I only heard a dull clunk as her shoes knocked against the wood. I couldn't see a thing. Everything fell silent.

As I was leaving I bumped into a priest. I greeted him with: "Christ be praised," then added: "Everyone's gone." He entered the church. A moment later the lights went out, I heard the sound of a key being turned, and a dark figure moved off quickly toward the presbytery.

WASYL PADWA

Wasyl Padwa was poor. He never ate a hot meal—so said the people that remembered him. Bright golden-colored tubs of jam would be standing on the counter in the store. Bread was delivered twice a week. Padwa didn't have anyone. He grazed the herd of cows that belonged to the PGR, the collective farm. At dawn in the summer the meadows are leaden and glisten like mercury. The sun still smells of underground coolness. Wasyl's rubber boots shone like officer's boots as he moved among the cattle, warming himself in the cloud of ruddy-colored heat. It may have been from the spectacle of boundless silver that he grew obsessed with one insistent thought: to be rich, to have more than he'd had up till now.

He ate less and less. His denim clothing turned grayer and grayer, and hung so loose it could have fit two of him.

*

Once a month a hunchbacked Warszawa would pull up in front of the store, and there, in the cherry-red glow from jars of conserves, amid the smell of raw bacon, beneath the eyes of the man in the fez on the Turek ersatz coffee tin, the cashier would lick his finger slowly and give him his wages. The shop clerk would make the same gesture as she turned the pages of her credit ledger, taking back what was hers and what was the government's. Wasyl Padwa always stood at the very end of the line, as if he was afraid someone might look over his shoulder, cast a spell on his growing treasure, or with a look erase one of the two zeros written by his name.

The banknotes, bearing a fisherman, a factory worker, or a miner, reminded him of postcards from distant lands. Sea, factory, mine—these were things he only knew from stories. Those who went there never came back. They disappeared like adventurers searching for El Dorado.

He would take his small wad of bills, fold it in two, then stow it in his inside button-up pocket, and people would laugh and say he didn't take his suit off even when he went to bed. He didn't drink, didn't smoke, didn't buy drinks for others. He left at sunrise with the cows, vanishing into the white mist.

Then one July there was a storm. The guys mowing hay ran down into the valley and took shelter wherever they could. Wasyl stayed up on the mountain, near the edge of the Sweet Woods. The cows stood out in the rain, their heads lowered, while he squatted under a hazel bush. The thunder licked at the peaks as usual, striking now here, now there; loose windowpanes rattled in the houses, and the purple flare of lightning made the children's faces look like someone was taking pictures of fear.

At that moment an old shed with a thatched roof caught fire. It stood high up on the meadows, right by the woods. People said later that Wasyl had run so fast it was like the wind was carrying him along; he rushed toward the shed through the lightning and rain. But storms are always more fire than water, and before he got there the thatch had turned into a red banner; then it split apart and collapsed. Wasyl's riches, hidden for years under the roof, burned along with the swifts' nests. Hundreds that were the color of the fire, fifties green as water, and twenties as gray as smoke.

*

But that isn't the end of the story, because true love is untouched even by fire. Wasyl Padwa began again from nothing. Now he changed all his banknotes into coins. Silver ones with a fisherman, and faded brown ones with Kościuszko and Copernicus. He went about jangling, then from time to time he'd stop making noise and everyone thought he must be burying his riches somewhere. But he had a simple, open nature, and since he'd suffered at the hands of fire, he decided to place his trust in water. Under Banne Hill there's a stream that twists and turns like a snake, and flows like a green carpet down cracked steps. It contains many dark and deep places. He put tens and fives in an old jam jar and lowered it gently into the current. The metallic disks reminded him of medals from long-ago wars. Some days the store clerk would chase him away, so he'd walk three miles to another store and there he'd exchange his paper phantoms for indestructible ore.

Then one summer there were such terrible rains you couldn't see further than ten feet. Wasyl's creek, which normally you could jump over in a single bound, carried off trees, set boulders rolling, and its waters grew thick with dull-colored mud. Wasyl Padwa waited day and night by the bank for it to return to its former course and turn clear again. But he found nothing aside from silt. Till autumn he walked up and down the bank searching for his hoard. The rocks had the faded hue of Copernicuses, and baby trout glinted in the sun like silver fives. He wandered up and down the bank the whole time till the fall, and the herd of cows, which naturally he couldn't leave untended, turned the meadow there into barren earth.

*

The third time, Wasyl Padwa entrusted his treasure to the earth. He chose a hiding place somewhere in the Sweet Woods. This story is the least clear of all. The exact place was known only to him and the person who discovered it after a year and stole his money. People laughed as they always do, and Padwa, who had finally grown tired of the elements, became the same as everyone else.

SUNDAY

There're only a few trees growing here. On scorching days it can be hard to find shade. In the afternoons a torrid light pours into every crevice like water. It's like a flood, and when it comes they take shelter under a young ash tree up on the hill. The earth they sit on is bare and worn like an old piece of furniture.

It all starts after Mass. The priest drives away in his tiny Fiat, while the rest of them walk a mile and a half down a dusty road. At ten in the morning the shadows are longer than the people, and cling to their left legs. They sit in a loose circle; they confer, and in the end two of them go to the little store a few dozen yards away. They buy cheap fruit wine, borrow a glass, get cigarettes as well. The sky is hard and unblemished, and the wine is called Di'Abolo.

At noon they can barely fit on their island of shade. When they go to bring successive bottles, the gold buckles on their shoes and the silver chains around their necks heat up as if in a fire, and everything around is swathed in a brightness such as some people see at the moment of their death: great empty cattle sheds, a black windowless house, fences, fields of nettles, the horizon, white shacks under blood-red roof tiles, children running with metal hoops, dogs, laundry hanging dead on the line, dust trailing behind a motorcycle, and all the other everyday things, licked by an invisible flame. Objects quiver, ripple, and look as if their moments are numbered. They're like grainy moving photographs in which there's more blackness than light.

But the men don't see any of this, because the vertical rays have already entered their skulls, and inside things are the same as outside. One of them says to another, "You go get more this time." "No. This time you go." Eventually one of them rises and moves off. He is utterly dark against the background of the sky. The wine is called Di'Abolo. It has a red, black, and orange label.

If at three in the afternoon they call you over to have a drink with them, don't be certain it's actually you they're calling. When you sit down among them it'll turn out they were talking to someone else entirely.

Then it's evening and sleep catches up with them in mid-sentence or mid-gesture. They assume old, preferred poses: on their back, on their side, curled into a ball. They look a bit like travelers who've forgotten to make a campfire. When the sun dips behind the crest of the hill, they'll start to cool down like the rest of the world, and soon their white shirts will be the only bright things in the pale blue light of dusk.

Toward the end their children appear. They poke about among the bodies in search of small change. They gather the empty bottles and exchange them in the store for orangeade.

RITE OF SPRING

When the frogs come out from beneath the earth and set off in search of standing water, it's a sign that winter has grown weak. White tongues of snow still lie in dark gullies, but their days are numbered. The streams are bursting with water, its animated, monotonous sound can be heard even through the walls of the house. Of the four elements, only earth has no voice of its own.

But this was supposed to be about the frogs, not the elements. So then, they crawl out of their hiding places and make their way to ditches and puddles, to stagnant, warmer water. Their bodies look like clods of glistening clay. If the day is sunny the meadow comes to life: dozens, hundreds of frogs moving up the slope. Actually it can barely be seen, for the color of their skin matches the dull hue of last year's grass. The eye catches only light and motion. They're still cold and half asleep, so they hop slowly, with long rests between bursts of effort. When the sun is shining at a particular angle, their journey is a series of brief flashes. They light up and go out again like will-o'-the-wisps in the middle of the day. But even now they join into pairs. Frogs' blood, as everyone knows, has the same temperature as the rest of the world, so as they push through patches of shadow on a clear but frost-sprinkled early morning, it's quite possible that red ice is flowing in their veins. Yet even now, one is seeking another, and they cling to each other in their strange two-headed, eight-legged way that makes Tosia call out: "Look! One frog's carrying the other one!"

*

All this is happening in a roadside ditch. The sun warms the water all day long, it's only in the late afternoon that the leafless willows cast an irregular network of shadows. There's no outflow here, it's sheltered from the wind, no stream runs into it, yet the surface of the water is dense with life. It's like the back of a great snake: it shimmers and coruscates, reflecting the light; the cold gleam slithers, melts away, divides, and does not come to a rest even for a moment.

To begin with it's only the frogs. Some are dark brown, almost black, with tiger stripes on their pale yellow legs. Others are bigger, the color of dusty fired clay—the ones in the water turn slightly red, take on warmer tones, and you can tell they're made of flesh.

Pairs join into foursomes, lone frogs adhere to couples, then there are eights, dozens, frog-balls appear with untold numbers of legs. They look like bizarre animals from the beginning of time, when the familiar forms of life had not yet been established, and the material expression of existence was still an experiment.

Soon frogspawn appears. At first it's clear as condensed water, then there's more and more of it and it acquires a luminous dark blue sheen. The water disappears completely, the inert shapeless substance reaches all the way to the bottom of the ditch, and when the frogs are startled by the shadow of an approaching human they dive in clumsily and only with effort. The substance, slimy and mercuric in its weight and its inertness, pushes them back to the surface. All this is accompanied by a sound that recalls an underwater rumbling of the belly.

*

When everything is over, the sky remains blue across its whole breadth. The surface of the water is equally still. The frogs have left, all that remains is the spawn and the bodies of those that didn't survive. They float up on their backs, they have white bellies, while pale pink filaments of intestine unravel from their mouths like some delicate species of water plant. This is the sign that spring has now arrived.

A LITTLE-USED ROOM

They appear in the house in late fall. The greatest number are in the attic. Some of them freeze into stillness and wait for the spring; others, the older ones, simply fall asleep and fail to wake up. The brown of their wings is downy and lusterless. The yellow of their peacock eyes has the warmth and brightness you can see in the windows of country cottages as a clear frosty dusk is falling, when it looks as if pieces of the burning western sky have been mounted in the frames.

The European Peacock butterfly, with wings made of pine bark (the kind that children use to make toy boats) that the sun has burned holes in. The edges are black, carbonized, while all around the prick-marks from the sun there's a glittering lilac-and-blue shimmer. It's the color metal takes on when it's fired to white heat then cooled; the rainbow becomes fixed in it, the temperature having permanently diffracted the light.

Some of them get into a room that's cold and rarely used. But it's enough to light the fire for a rustling sound to start up in the corners. They try to rise from the floor, from the dust and darkness. These creatures of air and light can be heard making a gray, powdery sound. The strongest ones occasionally fly up and flap toward the window.

Outside it's cold, the whiteness extends into infinity, yet they knock stubbornly against the pane. If they were let out, the frost would cut them down in a second, the way a candle flame will destroy a moth in the blink of an eye.

They die in a flutter of wings, in the cold sun of December. The sound has something of the susurration made by paper that's crumbling with age—if you rub it between your fingers it disintegrates into tiny pieces.

Eventually the sun sets, the room cools, dusk falls, and everything goes silent. Then they can be examined closely. The texture of the undersurface of their folded wings is like a fine mineral. The dark blue is shot through with black veins, while here and there you can see flecks of gold like those in a lump of coal. This combination of minerality and light makes their death seem unreal: surely it's not possible for something basically untouched by time to come so abruptly to an end.

But aside from the whole ones lying calm and hunched on their side, in the dark nooks and crannies you can find dozens of single torn-off wings. This may have been suicide, or some ultimate kind of self-repudiation.

PARTY

When the wind blows at night, the darkness shifts and sounds have their shapes. They can't be seen, but they enter the ear like material objects. The inside of the skull must be as vast as the entire neighborhood in order for everything to fit.

He was about to toss his cigarette away and go back home when he heard something. Air was moving across the tops of the trees like a huge black kite. The branches tore open the taut covering and from its far side, somewhere by the narrow ravine or the top of the mountain, came scattered sounds. As if from over there, from under the sky, from the heart of the gloom, a frolicking band of children had run up with their calls and shouts and Indian war whoops. The sheet of the wind undulated, stretched, and all at once began to close up like a roller blind. He was left in a total vacuum. The air rushed off that way, reaching the mountaintop. He knew it from the heavy rumbling in the ancient beech trees there. A flurry ran across the crest and in a moment of stillness he heard a woman's piercing, hysterical laugh, which, as it reached its highest note, turned into a sob. Then other, similar voices joined in, and it was only the next blast of cold air that drove the stolen echo into the depths of the night. He flicked his cigarette butt away. The red spark vanished at once. He couldn't tell if it had fallen into the snow or if a gust had swept it out of sight.

At moments the wind lifted up from the earth, passing over the peaks of the mountains, high up and far away, and the roar never died down even for a moment, as if over there, at the invisible frontier of the sky, a waterfall had opened up—as if, in the new Flood, air would take the place of water.

Then he heard it again. A lot closer. About halfway down the mountainside. It was like a pack of dogs short of breath—that was what he thought to himself. Dogs whose barking had been thrust back down their throats by the wind, so the only sound they could make was a shrill, intermittent yelping. Dogs that were unable to bark. Then he heard one more sound and felt his skin crawl.

*

The next day he went there. The wind had stopped. The snow and mist had the color of milky glass. The trees looked like a detailed drawing on which water had been spilled. The blood had darkened already, but when he swept a little snow aside with the toe of his boot, he saw that underneath it was bright and live. He looked around. A broad, empty stretch of ground separated him from the woods. He thought to himself, come on, it's daytime, but he couldn't overcome his unease. He studied the tracks. This was where the animal had fallen, but it had still had the strength to get back up and keep running away. The marks of wolf paws were distinct. Tufts of dark brown fur with a gray underside had been left in the disturbed snow. The crows led the way from there.

It was a young doe. It looked like a discarded bundle of sticks and dirty rags. He found pulled-off bones with the remains of flesh still on them. The wolves had each taken their own share, gone off a little higher up, and eaten at a safe distance from one another, in a wide semicircle around their main course. Then they'd descended, taken another portion, and returned to their places. It had probably lasted till morning.

Now everything was so still it was as if nothing would ever happen here again. He thought about the nighttime commotion and remembered all those parties where people speak in raised voices, talking on top of one another, their hands occupied with gestures and silverware, and it's only the ironic light of dawn that brings calm.

He went back down. That was all the crows were waiting for.

CRAYFISH

The fish were dead already. The water had disappeared. The sky had burned itself a mirror in which it had been reflected for the last month. The bright, wan fire had reached the stones. It looked like a road made of white bones, something like that. The way wound across a ruddy-colored meadow, deep and absurdly convoluted, filled with the buzzing of flies. The willow green and ink-black insects had the hardness of metal, the mobility and gleam of mercury. Everything else—the air, the woods on the hillside, the buzzard circling around the sun—was motionless.

We walked up the creek. The rounded rocks gave out a wooden thud when they were kicked. The short sound started up, rose into the air, and immediately ceased. A dozen or so alders grew in a bend by the crag. In the place where the current had once dropped down a series of steps, there was silence. The puddles had the color of dirty bottle glass. Kamil said a beer would be good, and I answered that it'd be better to wait till evening, because it was pointless to drink and drink like that.

Then we saw them. Just the eyes. The round brown beads still retained their shine. The rest of their bodies had already come to resemble minerals. Their exoskeletons were covered with drying mud. They moved sluggishly, they didn't so much as try to get away. They simply retreated among the rocks, pulling their pincers behind them. A low scraping noise could be heard. They moved like weakened mechanisms, like wound-up toys about to fall still. Some were already motionless, like the rest of the river.

We went home. We took a child's pink toy pail. An open Gazik jeep drove down the road. The firefighters wore dark glasses and were naked to the waist. "A patrol," I said. "Right," answered Kamil, and we entered the cloud of hot dust from the car.

They didn't put up any resistance. We took them in our hands. They moved their pincers. They cut the dense, stinking air at an infinitely slow tempo. We threw them into the pail. They made a grating noise like a handful of pebbles. The dried-up creek entered a larger one that was still flowing. We went there. The water was cold and clear. Small trout were twisting in patches of sunlight. We dropped the crayfish in one by one. The small ones swam away at once, the larger ones sank slowly, their limbs spread wide, and came to rest without moving on the bottom. They became less gray. Now they resembled those kinds of shalelike stones that acquire a vivid, greenish color when you immerse them in water. Red showed through at their bent joints. They crawled slowly, stunned by the sudden chill; they paused, moved on, and eventually disappeared in the tangle of roots hanging from the bank. We went to get more, and then one more time again. On the way we found a slow worm. It was flat and stiff, completely dry. We picked out anything that moved. Even the tiny little ones no bigger than grasshoppers.

In the evening we went for that beer. The sun was done for the day and had gone behind the mountain, leaving strips of red like scraps of meat in the sky. The firefighters were also drinking.

Later, the other creek dried up too.

BIRDS

In winter no one walked that road.

January was sunny and almost snowless. We were plodding along up to our ankles and Wasyl said, "Look at them all in a huddle."

Before we reached them they flew off. Crows, white-beaked rooks, ravens, chattering jays, and jays with their wings touched with pale blue.

And some smaller kinds. In the place they took off from we found a deer.

In place of its eyes it had red cavities in a smooth white frame of bone.

Wasyl looked for the wound that had killed it, but the skin was torn in many places. Tufts of drab fur were scattered here and there.

"Maybe it dropped dead, maybe it was shot," he said, and we walked back.

*

A week later we returned to the same place. From far off you could hear the warning screech of the magpies. Last to fly off was a raven. We heard the air whistle between its flight feathers.

The deer had become a complex white structure. Its ribs spanned an empty place and resembled beams, the rafters of some hall or hangar. I thought of the pavilions at the World's Fair, perhaps the one in Osaka, or somewhere else. There was no trace of flesh, no trace of blood, just clumps of hair blown by the wind to the edge of the undergrowth a few yards away. Dry thistles decorated with brown and white fluff.

"Look," said Wasyl, kicking at the snow around the skeleton. His boot slipped on the solid white shell. Birds' feet had trampled the powdery snow like a threshing floor, into white rock. Even inside, under the tent of bones, it was hard and glistening. Skeleton and snow had fused into a single whole. In a nearby grove of young pines the crows and magpies flapped from branch to branch, waiting for us to be done marveling at their weight.

STORKS

They appeared at the beginning of April, when frogs were already starting to teem in the stagnant ponds. The dusk had been mild, wisps of cloud speeding southward. The weather turned in the night.

In the morning almost a hundred of them had gathered. In the gray sleet they looked like remnants of snow, they could barely be told apart from the patches of dirty white that lingered in ditches and under bushes. They stood motionless, given away only by the red of their bills and legs. Moisture was freezing on the bare branches. The tiniest blade of grass was encased in a little sheath of ice. From time to time one of the birds would spread its wings.

I couldn't hear it, but the awkward flapping must have been accompanied by a crunching sound. The hardiest of them wandered toward puddles. They shuffled about on the ice. The half-asleep frogs were less than an inch away.

By evening nothing had changed. The wind brought alternating waves of snow and drizzle.

The next day it was even colder. That kind of wind in winter always brings a snowstorm. From time to time the towering ring of clouds cracked open from end to end, and for a moment there appeared blue sky or a glint of sun; then darkness set in again.

The strongest ones tried to fly, making a long run-up and an unnaturally quick ascent into the wind, then dropped immediately, like failed paper airplanes. When the gale eased a little, they would shift a couple hundred yards farther on, then settle amid equally frozen pools of water. And though there were alder thickets close by, not one of them took shelter there.

At dawn on the third day the wind died down and the sun came out. I didn't see them fly away. One was left behind. It looked like an overturned plaything.

GREEN LACEWINGS

"My mother used to call them 'glass bugs,'" said Wieś, blowing the insect from his hand.

We would come across them from time to time over the summer. They possessed a beauty rare among the hymenopterans. Their transparent wings were a delicate yet at the same time vivid shade of green. Their eyes were not at all golden, despite their Polish name of *złotook* or "gold-eye." Rather, they looked like flecks of copper, or the eyes of lizards. In full sunlight, the juxtaposition of the two colors created an impression of extraordinary purity: metal, precious stone, and light. The glare passed through them; they barely cast any shadow.

As they crawled across the table they tested the way with their curving feelers. Most of all they liked scattered sugar granules. Perhaps they were attracted to forms resembling their own.

As autumn progressed they began to gather in the house. At that time it turned out that, as well as belonging to the mineral realm, there was also something about them that linked them to the world of plants. As there was less and less sunlight, the green of their wings began to fade. By November they looked like a precision drawing made with the finest pencil.

In the evenings, when we lit candles, these scarcely visible sketches would flutter from dark corners, from crevices in the wooden walls, and speed toward the flames, till in a final flare even their outline was lost.

THE SWALLOWS

At the beginning of September everything changed. It was exactly as if the sky had an inside. Early one morning the blue burst and released a wind mixed with an icy downpour.

It was perfect weather for vodka. The house shook from the gusts, the roof trusses creaked like the hull of a sailing ship. We rocked to and fro, it took great effort not to spill even a drop from the tiny brimming glass. We drank to the cold and to the wind.

From the north came drops of rain like drab threads; they vanished somewhere to the south without touching the ground at all. In this dull-colored blizzard all shapes disappeared. The woods and the river could be told by the increasing roar. But it was quite possible they'd both been swept away and were hurtling some-where across the world, tangled in a ball.

"Like it was let off its leash," said Wieś. He probably meant the air.

The next day the swallows appeared. They were always there and so we paid no attention to them. But their numbers . . . Two, three, ten times as many as usual. They flew ponderously just above the ground, like they were trying to avoid the wind, to escape from it, hide. Some of them hung beneath the eaves, their claws latched to the wall. That was the only dry place.

The following morning we found their dead bodies. They weighed next to nothing. It was then we understood how much strength a bundle of feathers like that has to have to ride out a gale.

The rain didn't ease up even for a moment.

In the afternoon we cracked open a window. Five swallows flew into the house. They settled on the stove, close to the ceiling. We were able to take them in the palms of our hands. They made no attempt to fly away. The tiny drumbeat of their hearts was un-imaginably fast.

The next morning was sunny. We let the birds out. We gathered the dead bodies scattered around the outside of the house. When the fire was going, we put them gently into the stove.

THE RIVER

We were exhausted. Animals and humans. The heat wave had gone on for two months. July and August melted into a liquid double month, while we floundered in that interminably long, torrid time like flies in a jar of honey. The sun would disappear over the horizon, yet its swelter lingered till dawn. It was extinguished only by the dew that came down an hour before sunrise.

We tried to drink beer, but it refreshed only for a brief, sickly moment, then plunged us back into lethargy.

"Goddamn metabolism," Wieś would say, and shake his head to another bottle. We would go back home along the bank of the river, which with every day looked more and more like a road paved with white rocks. No birds could be heard in the bushes. Discolored yellowhammers stirred little clouds of dust on the path. The distant trees, the bluffs, and the great stone cross on the hill took on a supernatural distinctness. The transparency of the air increased the dimensions of the world, but our gaze, whetted on the sharply defined edges of objects, still seemed to retain complete control over it. And then there were the insects. Despite the windless weather the air quivered constantly. Green and blue dragonflies, wasps and hornets, bumblebees and damselflies infused the motionless landscape with an imperceptible, oppressive resonance.

In the bleached grass we would find torpid frogs. Their goldtinted pupils were glazed, their skin had lost its luster. Soon we began to step on their bodies. Swollen and dry, they made a noise like little boxes of thin, stiff cardboard.

One day—it would have been early afternoon, since we were on our way back from our single beer—we saw that the river had disappeared. "Look," said Wieś, and we immediately left the path. The riverbed looked like a white scar. Flies stirred amid the burning hot rocks. We smelled the stench of rotting fish. The last live ones were writhing in muddy pools. The sky had the look of hard, pale blue porcelain.

Nothing disturbed the cruelty of that moment.

RAIN

At five in the morning it started raining again. The first drops hit the rocks with the soft sound of bursting flesh. The glare of dawn was still glowing over the black rim of the mountain and the downpour was filled with silvery light. But it only lasted a moment. The covering of cloud moved along soundlessly, its woolly edge could be seen from below, then things went back to normal. For weeks now we'd been in a strange world where light had no strength. It lurked in corners, tried to detach itself from the surface of things, but it was as if objects were magnetized. They'd not only absorbed the glare; they themselves were also slowly disappearing, shrinking, collapsing in on themselves. In the middle of the day you had to light a lamp in order to find them.

We watched the gray comb of the drizzle grooming the bushes. The tall grasses lay down on their sides, while the water seeped between the blades into spongy earth, murmuring in the tunnels of insects and mice, finding its way to underground lakes that swelled and rose with every day. Dark mirrors began to shine on the flat meadows. But they reflected nothing. Every last shard of glow had gone from the air. True, the landscape was still in place, but its colors had all grown more alike, and the whole world was now somewhere between black and leaden green.

We were slowly disappearing too. Cigarettes, one coffee after another—nothing did any good. Our blood had been thinned. It flowed ever more slowly. One day I cut my finger, and what came out was a transparent liquid like the sap of a plant. After all, people are made up mostly of water, and two weeks of rain are enough for their bodies to turn back into what they used to be at the beginning. Watery dust, mist, and drizzle had soaked through the skin and remained inside. Even vodka, usually volatile and hot, now burned up in the veins with a sorry hiss: the glass was like a damp match, and that was that.

In the short moments at dawn or before sunset when the sky brightened, the light took on a sickly intensity. At these times it expanded abruptly and sought release. A rumbling and whistling could be heard, and the tattered edges of the clouds glowed orange. But it only ever lasted a moment, then the murmuring, sodden gloom set in once again.

One day the mailman came in a waterproof overcoat. The envelopes were limp as wet handkerchiefs. "Everything's damp," he said. "It's wet when it gets to us." Nothing was legible. The words must have melted away even before they were written. At that point we lost whatever hope we still had.

END OF SEPTEMBER

Once through the gate you turn right. The village lane is narrow, it runs along the bank of the creek. After the rains the water has the color of lusterless emerald with an undertone of silt. The houses are mostly wooden, from before the war. They have glassed-in verandas. When someone slams a door, the small rectangular panes rattle like in an old dresser. Footbridges hidden in the bushes lead to the houses on the other side of the creek. In gaps between the tall trees you can see the mountains. Their distant, essentially decorative presence gives the lane something of the look of a resort or a fairy tale. At the end there's a preschool. That's why you mostly meet children there, and a black-and-white dog. On sunny days the place is mostly plunged in shade interspersed with a trembling greenish glow in which a golden light is diluted as if in water, and at such moments the air becomes visible. The borderline where the atmosphere meets people and objects is softened. It's like an innocent attempt at proving the primal unity of all things.

But with the end of September everything changes. It's enough to leave the house and walk twenty yards, and instead of a country alleyway, instead of an avenue of old trees there's just an inferno, columns of fire and blazing bushes. The flames rise from the depths of the earth and, coming up through the thick trunks of sycamore and linden and chestnut, burst into the sky like fiery feather headdresses. If a wind is blowing, the air is filled with smoldering scraps. Even the dark elderberries, which look like polished pieces of coal, seem to be alight, as if they held glowing embers in their moist interiors. Leaves spin, drop into the water with a hiss and turn to ash. After the first frosts the wild vine turns red and runs down the walls of houses like thick blood.

At eight on a Tuesday morning temptation emerges from every corner. The cigarette has the same taste as always, children roll about like colored balls, milk cans rattle, nothing changes, but everything suggests that the soul is a fiction of the mind, which is trying to use it to equal the visible world. Yet it's all in vain, because even thought vanishes in the incandescent aura of early morning. The sky is blue, distant, cold. Sparks crackle along the rusty wire fences. Yellow explosions, crimson, slanting rays melting and spilling into the air like golden wax, magma and malignant fever, fear and trembling, the praise and glory of matter whose red tongue is licking reality down to the bone.

FROST

In the night the temperature fell to twenty-two below. A round moon hung beneath the dark blue vault of the sky and it all resembled a dream in which the outlines of events leading us into temptation can barely be made out. We know it's perilous, but we don't want to wake up.

The air hung in place, strained to its limits, and not a single sound could hide in it. Noises that usually would fall silent after a moment now went on without end, because a frost like that makes even time freeze solid, fusing it with light and air. This newly produced substance had the resonant quality of metal.

We were walking along an old logging road that had been smoothed over by sleds hauling timber. The tiniest things cast a shadow. A lump of ice, the track left by a runner, the imprint of a winter horseshoe, a broken branch—everything had its own black double. The bark of the beech trees shone with a glassy burnish. White, silver, and black entered into subtle combinations with one another, thus placing reality under a question mark. And if not reality, then at least the purpose and meaning of perception. The landscape breathed death: the rivers had frozen solid, birds were dying in flight, and the woods resounded with the crack of splitting trees. That sound was pitiless, because the silence lengthened it into infinity. The hard, dead snap endured in space as in eternity, endured as an ideal model of hopeless sorrow.

Then the road ended and we came out by a scarcely trodden path onto an exposed pass.

Down below lay the earth. It was turned on its back, spread-eagled, given over to icy light. An unseen immobility seeped down from the heavens, filling the crannies, the hollows in trees, the holes beneath the bark, the crevices in the rocky cliffs above Zawoja, the insides of the trees, the bodies of animals, the skin of humans, the porous structure of stones, walls, houses, blades of dry grass, straw mulch around plants, stocks of food, dogs' kennels, cats' baskets in attics, thoughts, dreams and fears before falling asleep—everything lost its fluid nature, shifting toward immutability, toward the fulfillment of dreams, in the direction of the place where alpha entwines with omega, and essence creeps into existence like the delicious tingling in the feet and hands felt by a drunk in the frost.

The snow shone with a luciferous shimmer. Temptation always assumes an aesthetic form. The stars were dim glittering pinpricks. Things that are unencompassable, indifferent, and beautiful draw us to their rim and perhaps watch as we sway at the edge of the abyss, touched in equal part by desire and fear. The mercuric moonlight grew ever colder, trembling in the valley at our feet. The vividness of the dark landscape surpassed its realness. We heard dogs. The barking came from the south, but there were no villages there, and so the sound must have been circling amid the frozen expanses of air like an acoustic fata morgana. It was quite possible that the concentrated space had preserved these noises since the previous winter, and that our faint, half-whispered conversation would also be kept, and we'd be heard by others a year or a century later. In the end, by an effort of will, we forced ourselves to push on. There was something cowardly in this motion of ours. We were slipping out the back way, a little like scurrying animals intent on preserving a modicum of heat in their tiny bodies, while the rest of the world was simply enduring in its magnificent prodigal way.

RAIN IN DECEMBER

On Monday it began to rain. For several days there'd been a thaw. We were on our way home. Darek cursed, turned the wheel, and the car skidded on wet ice. We tried to use the sides of the road, where there were rocks sticking up. The way was clear, straight, climbing gently for four or five miles. The houses on both sides looked abandoned. Their windows reflected blackness, though the sky was the color of dirty water. A motorcycle was coming down the hill. The rider was sliding along the sheer surface, his feet spread wide. He looked like a stiff horseman whose mount had suddenly shrunk to the size of a WSK motorbike.

We crawled higher. The village was left behind. The rain was trying to wipe it off the map. A mile before the pass Darek said, "Dammit, it's raining and freezing." The windshield wipers were scraping against the glass like they were trying to get inside the car.

Then we came to the woods: it was strange, translucent, like something from a dream. Young alders leaned over the road. Their crowns rubbed against the roof of the car. Elder bushes, pussy willow, hazel trees, all spread like clumps of silvery seaweed frozen still in their underwater swaying. Everything was covered in ice. Every branch, every tiniest blade of grass was sheathed in a transparent cover. Once, long ago, they sold colored candies in glass tubes with a stopper at one end. It was a little like that: glass tubes, and in each one a stalk, a twig, even the pine needles had been dressed individually, with great care. A blackthorn plunged in ice looked like a living corporeal being surprised by the flash of an X-ray.

We pulled over. We'd never seen anything like it. The snow was covered by a hard skin. Drops of rain fell with a soft rattling sound. Trees were bent every which way in the motionless air. The tips of the huge firs by the pass leaned toward one another in a puppetlike dance. It was exactly as though a great wind had passed over the area and had suddenly come to a halt. It had ceased, but had kept on blowing. It had stopped dead in place. I thought to myself that the feathers of birds, if there were any birds at all that day, must be making a crunching sound in flight, from their icy carapace.

We drove on. The gray-green trunks of the young ashes had the glassy shine of man-made things.

It rained all night. The world seemed about to turn into an icicle. It seemed about to become like one of those glass spheres containing a little house and a snowman, with little flakes falling from a blue sky. Only the loud roar in the darkness clashed with that image.

NIGHT

It looks as if it was rocking a moment ago, and it was only your gaze that stopped it moving. A blade, or a shaving from a silver disk, hanging above the hump of Ubocze Mountain like one side of a curved pair of shears over a sheep's back, or like a hook right by the mouth of a big fish. It's the first night of the first quarter of October, when the moon has barely an hour in the sky. Then it's swallowed up by the earth near Grybów and you're left alone in the darkness.

You can't see your own hand, or other people, you can't see the things whose shape existence usually takes, you can't even see the air moving between your fingers. To believe in your own life you have to take hold of yourself, or escape into memory. Without the world, without the variety of forms all around, a person is naught but a mirror in which nothing is reflected. During the day this cannot be seen, because light is thinner and more weightless than air. It sneaks into every crevice, which is to say all shapes—the tangible, the visible, and at times the invisible too. Now things are different. The primal matter of the dark enters the veins and circulates like blood.

Somewhere a dog barks. In their houses, people make the day last longer with lamps and television sets. They want to see their lives, their objects, all they've accumulated between their four walls since the beginning of the world, since the time they made the first fire. From above, from very far up, the towns and villages look like the remains of campfires.

In the beginning was darkness and now, at six forty in the evening in 1996, the oldest time is in progress. In my pocket I have Marlboro cigarettes and other things that people carry with them at the end of the twentieth century, but if it weren't for the vagaries of memory I'd only be a piece of matter barely brought to life and plunged into the dark of ages. It's quite possible that the body is a warm, compact variety of darkness, and that at moments such as this one the night is simply reaching out to claim its own. The black extends into infinity. Nothing greater comes to mind. This is what a droplet must feel like when it falls into water.

The remnants of the glow over Ubocze fade soundlessly and the mountain disappears in a gulf of dark blue. The village of Ropa reminds you of a legend about a drowned world in which, in order to see anything, people have to emit their own light.

Darkness and time—weightless, invisible substances that expose human frailty. The mind is nothing but a match flame in the wind. The soul cowers in the body from fear of the gloom, while the body double-checks its existence by touching its own skin. And so in the end what remains is that simplest of the senses, thanks to which insects crawl in the earth, and we can distinguish what's living from what's dead, and very little else.

BEYOND THE THRESHOLD

It's enough to cross the threshold. The open door lets out the warmth of the house, the smell of cigarettes and food; the calm aroma of the last few hours enters the turmoil of the southern wind. In this way life combines with the rest of the world and the circle closes. It's the same with other people. The ephemeral infusions of their presence pass through loose windows, old walls, rotten floorboards, and join with the primal kingdom of the elements. Oxygenium, Natrium, Hydrogenium, Nitrogenium, Ferrum . . . First comes the stale warmth of living rooms, then cold gusts along country lanes, air masses over Ubocze Mountain, the stratosphere, and the constellations; it makes my head spin as I inhale it all deep into my lungs a few minutes after midnight, while everyone else is sleeping and utterly indifferent to the fact that they're circulating among states of concentration.

So then I cross the threshold, there's a full moon and I can see all the way to Chełm Mountain, whose top looks like an animal moving at a steady trot, and I know that nothing extraordinary is circulating in my veins or settling in my bones. Ferrum, Calcium . . . The same as in the black skeletons of fences, the ruins of cellars out in the wasteland, in the river beneath the ice and in the ice itself, sliced up by the skates of children, who also contain the same thing; whichever way you turn, whatever mental somersault you perform, still everything returns to its primal form, which iridesces, turns shapes inside out, and pulls the mind by its hair to get it to reflect everything like a mirror.

So I go back, close the door, and sit at the table, but a quarter of an hour later uncertainty impels me out again and I go check whether this is really how things are.

The constellations are turning and sprinkling light on the houses. The sharp rooftops slice the glow in two, and it falls and soaks into the earth like rain. And there's nothing else in this landscape except the light; I'm looking for evidence of my separateness, but in the middle of the night, when everyone else is asleep, it can't be found. So I retreat one more time, in order with the aid of coffee and a cigarette—those indubitable signs of humanity—to get a grip on myself. And only two minutes later I'm ensconced in an armchair like the crown of creation, the ashtray within easy reach.

But the elements and the groups of stars were in cahoots, and they rubbed temptingly against the windowpane and the vast space above the village in an attempt to lure me out and deprive me of salvation, because it wasn't about the beauty of the Gorlice region but about the existence of the soul as an insubstantial substance not included in the periodic table of the elements. It was about whether I would derive being from nonbeing, or if I would equal nonbeing with being and the cosmos would swallow the logos the way a goose swallows a noodle.

And I didn't go out a third time, because I was overcome by fear. To put it differently: I'd lost my nerve. For how can the invisible be distilled from the visible except by a perilous experiment involving, with all due respect, the integrity of one's own coherence?

SKY

When all else has passed, there'll still remain the sky that spreads now over the town of Dukla, over the village of Łosie, over southern Poland, over the whole world. There won't be people anymore, but this image of the human soul, human intelligence, human essence, will endure in time that's slowly turning into eternity, till in the end it too disappears like everything else. In any case there's one sure consolation: the Image, twin brother of our mind, will outlive us.

On certain days the meteorological metaphor moves toward an actual representation. At such times the swollen matter of the clouds resembles the folds of the human brain. Windless, warm, damp weather forms water vapor into regular coils and infuses them with the grayish purple light of tedium. In these moments we pace from wall to wall, bouncing around the inside of the house, our mind taking leave of our head yet finding only itself.

Or when the wind blows from the east and drives air masses from over Ukraine, Siberia, and Alaska, propelling them around the world, and the clouds tear apart, burst, form together again, no shape lasting more than a moment and none repeating, just as there are never two waves alike on the ocean, nor two snowflakes in winter; yet the chaos is universal in scope and what is happening over Tokarnia and Berd and Ubycze is merely a fragment of the atmosphere of the entire globe, though even this tiny instance is enough to grasp the fact that the madness, mutability, and infinity of forms ends up acquiring a cosmic monotony and is reminiscent of the human mind, whose freedom and mobility tend toward stupefaction and terror, in the moment when it comprehends that all that was merely play, merely chasing one's own tail. The former collective farm of Moszczaniec to the left continues its unreal existence, and we're running on empty. The nearest gas station isn't till Komańcza.

Or when the sun is setting and the edges of the clouds look like wounds. The road from Tylawa climbs to the crest of Słonna Mountain and the entire south burns like an allegory of atrocity. Blood is bright, it shines with its own glow. The view brings to mind all those things we desire and are afraid of, because gold is always light, and red always blood and fire, which is to say the most enticing forms of death. Of course, driving down to Załuże we're moving on the borderline of good taste. But we cannot avoid the horror that comes when the senses open themselves to the infinite. Time is only an idea, while space alas resembles a fact. That's why it agitates the imagination, which does in fact consider itself to be boundless, but doesn't actually exist. Luckily, immediately afterward we come to Sanok.

Or high, bright afternoons. At these times the blue looks like painted glass. Hot air rises from the bottom of the Ciechań and between Czumak and Czerteż you won't see a living soul. There are only adders warming themselves on the old gray roadway. But they're merely flesh, as everyone knows. And if a weather front happens to be passing through, in the chasmic depths of the blueness long white clouds will show up. They look like bones, like a scattered and hazy vertebral column. Because that's how things will be at the very end. Even the clouds will vanish and all that will remain will be an endless blue eye hovering over the ruins.

ANDRZEJ STASIUK has received numerous awards for his work, including the NIKE, Poland's most prestigious literary prize, for his collection of essays *On the Road to Babadag*. His novel *Nine* was published in English to great acclaim in 2007.

BILL JOHNSTON is the leading translator of Polish literature in the United States. His translation of Tadeusz Różewicz's *new poems* won the 2008 Found in Translation Award and was a finalist for the National Book Critics Circle Poetry Award.

SELECTED DALKEY ARCHIVE PAPERBACKS

FOR A FULL LIST OF PUBLICATIONS, VISIT:
www.dalkeyarchive.com

Man in the Holocene.
CARLOS FUENTES, *Christopher Unborn.*
Distant Relations.
Terra Nostra.
Where the Air Is Clear.
WILLIAM GADDIS, *J R.*
The Recognitions.
JANICE GALLOWAY, *Foreign Parts.*
The Trick Is to Keep Breathing.
WILLIAM H. GASS, *Cartesian Sonata and Other Novellas.*
Finding a Form.
A Temple of Texts.
The Tunnel.
Willie Masters' Lonesome Wife.
GÉRARD GAVARRY, *Hoppla! 1 2 3.*
Making a Novel.
ETIENNE GILSON,
The Arts of the Beautiful.
Forms and Substances in the Arts.
C. S. GISCOMBE, *Giscome Road.*
Here.
Prairie Style.
DOUGLAS GLOVER, *Bad News of the Heart.*
The Enamoured Knight.
WITOLD GOMBROWICZ,
A Kind of Testament.
KAREN ELIZABETH GORDON,
The Red Shoes.
GEORGI GOSPODINOV, *Natural Novel.*
JUAN GOYTISOLO, *Count Julian.*
Exiled from Almost Everywhere.
Juan the Landless.
Makbara.
Marks of Identity.
PATRICK GRAINVILLE, *The Cave of Heaven.*
HENRY GREEN, *Back.*
Blindness.
Concluding.
Doting.
Nothing.
JACK GREEN, *Fire the Bastards!*
JIŘÍ GRUŠA, *The Questionnaire.*
GABRIEL GUDDING,
Rhode Island Notebook.
MELA HARTWIG, *Am I a Redundant Human Being?*
JOHN HAWKES, *The Passion Artist.*
Whistlejacket.
ALEKSANDAR HEMON, ED.,
Best European Fiction.
AIDAN HIGGINS, *A Bestiary.*
Balcony of Europe.
Bornholm Night-Ferry.
Darkling Plain: Texts for the Air.
Flotsam and Jetsam.
Langrishe, Go Down.
Scenes from a Receding Past.
Windy Arbours.
KEIZO HINO, *Isle of Dreams.*
KAZUSHI HOSAKA, *Plainsong.*
ALDOUS HUXLEY, *Antic Hay.*
Crome Yellow.
Point Counter Point.
Those Barren Leaves.
Time Must Have a Stop.
NAOYUKI II, *The Shadow of a Blue Cat.*
MIKHAIL IOSSEL AND JEFF PARKER, EDS.,
Amerika: Russian Writers View the United States.
DRAGO JANČAR, *The Galley Slave.*
GERT JONKE, *The Distant Sound.*

Geometric Regional Novel.
Homage to Czerny.
The System of Vienna.
JACQUES JOUET, *Mountain R.*
Savage.
Upstaged.
CHARLES JULIET, *Conversations with Samuel Beckett and Bram van Velde.*
MIEKO KANAI, *The Word Book.*
YORAM KANIUK, *Life on Sandpaper.*
HUGH KENNER, *The Counterfeiters.*
Flaubert, Joyce and Beckett: The Stoic Comedians.
Joyce's Voices.
DANILO KIŠ, *Garden, Ashes.*
A Tomb for Boris Davidovich.
ANITA KONKKA, *A Fool's Paradise.*
GEORGE KONRÁD, *The City Builder.*
TADEUSZ KONWICKI, *A Minor Apocalypse.*
The Polish Complex.
MENIS KOUMANDAREAS, *Koula.*
ELAINE KRAF, *The Princess of 72nd Street.*
JIM KRUSOE, *Iceland.*
EWA KURYLUK, *Century 21.*
EMILIO LASCANO TEGUI, *On Elegance While Sleeping.*
ERIC LAURRENT, *Do Not Touch.*
HERVÉ LE TELLIER, *The Sextine Chapel.*
A Thousand Pearls (for a Thousand Pennies)
VIOLETTE LEDUC, *La Bâtarde.*
EDOUARD LEVÉ, *Autoportrait.*
Suicide.
SUZANNE JILL LEVINE, *The Subversive Scribe: Translating Latin American Fiction.*
DEBORAH LEVY, *Billy and Girl.*
Pillow Talk in Europe and Other Places.
JOSÉ LEZAMA LIMA, *Paradiso.*
ROSA LIKSOM, *Dark Paradise.*
OSMAN LINS, *Avalovara.*
The Queen of the Prisons of Greece.
ALF MAC LOCHLAINN,
The Corpus in the Library.
Out of Focus.
RON LOEWINSOHN, *Magnetic Field(s).*
MINA LOY, *Stories and Essays of Mina Loy.*
BRIAN LYNCH, *The Winner of Sorrow.*
D. KEITH MANO, *Take Five.*
MICHELINE AHARONIAN MARCOM,
The Mirror in the Well.
BEN MARCUS,
The Age of Wire and String.
WALLACE MARKFIELD,
Teitlebaum's Window.
To an Early Grave.
DAVID MARKSON, *Reader's Block.*
Springer's Progress.
Wittgenstein's Mistress.
CAROLE MASO, *AVA.*
LADISLAV MATEJKA AND KRYSTYNA POMORSKA, EDS.,
Readings in Russian Poetics: Formalist and Structuralist Views.
HARRY MATHEWS,
The Case of the Persevering Maltese: Collected Essays.
Cigarettes.
The Conversions.
The Human Country: New and

FOR A FULL LIST OF PUBLICATIONS, VISIT:
www.dalkeyarchive.com

SELECTED DALKEY ARCHIVE PAPERBACKS

SELECTED DALKEY ARCHIVE PAPERBACKS

FOR A FULL LIST OF PUBLICATIONS, VISIT:
www.dalkeyarchive.com